BLOOD LUST!

I could hear screams of fear and anger, and more shots. More ponies were crowding me, and I smashed the butt of my Henry against a head that was looming over me. Reaching on around with my left hand, I got the Remington from my holster and triggered it into an Injun's face, till he threw his hands up and disappeared under my horse's hoofs. More guns were going off, and the acrid bite of powder smoke filled my eyes. A rage was building in me, a berserk urge to kill....

ROBERT BELL

Platte River Crossing

BALLANTINE BOOKS • NEW YORK

Library of Congress Catalog Card Number: 83-90028

ISBN 0-345-31208-2

Manufactured in the United States of America

First Edition: October 1983

CHAPTER 1

THEY'D STOPPED THE STAGE IN A GROVE OF COTtonwoods, and a horse was down, thrashing in a tangle of harness. Silently, I swore to myself. Damn a man who'd kill a horse without any good reason!

I counted four men in the gang. One was standing close to the front of the coach, a double gun leveled at the two men on the box. The messenger had his hands in the air, and his shotgun lay on the ground by the robber's feet. Old man Forney, the driver, sat slumped over in his seat, a dark and spreading stain on his left shoulder.

As I watched, two of the holdups dismounted and approached the stage, while the fourth remained on horseback, his rifle held at the ready. They were old hands at this game.

One man jerked the coach door open and motioned to those inside to come out. There were six passengers. The first man who stepped down turned back to offer his hand to a woman passenger, and she joined him on the ground. The other four were men, and they lined up with their hands held high.

Reaching down, I slid the Henry rifle from its scabbard and jacked a round into the chamber. Better I waited. With the passengers so close, it would be dangerous to risk a try at the robbers.

Believe it or not, I was here of my own free accord. Two days before, I'd been laying around the National Hotel lobby in Leavenworth, Kansas; money in my pocket and nothing more to do than to spend it. My friend, Charley Canfield, and I had shipped a trainload of cattle to Chicago and decided to take a few days' vacation. Charley was all for going back to Kansas City and the Muhlbach Hotel, there on Twelfth Street. He had him a young lady who thought the sun rose and set on middle-aged cattle buyers with a pocketful of *dinero*.

Me? A long ways from middle-age, I'd just turned twenty-

1

seven, and only last year I'd driven two big herds up from a ranch my folks and I had in southwest Texas. We'd sold them cattle to Canfield for a top price, and I'd decided to spend some time seeing the sights in Yankeeland.

Wasn't exactly free choice. I'd set my heart on marrying a girl back there in Texas, and she'd chosen my brother, who stayed behind. Busted me up some, and I'd told the others a big story about wanting to see the world. Sent them on back to Texas, my youngest brother, Lysander, in charge. Taken a small part of our sales money and asked Lysander to bank my share of what was left.

Canfield and I had taken the steam cars to Kansas City; a real treat for me because I'd never set foot on one. There weren't any more herds coming north, what with winter coming on, so Canfield had decided to leave Abilene and head east. While sitting there in the parlor car with drinks in our hands, I asked him his plans.

"Time I was getting on back to Chicago," he replied. "My two brothers and I have a business to run. How about yours, Rush? You've got a stake now. What do you intend to do?"

I mumbled something about not really knowing, and he sure was mighty quick to pick up on that!

"I need a man in Kansas City," he told me. "Someone that knows cattle and can handle men, also. Kansas City has big yard facilities, and sometimes we put cattle we've bought in feed lots there. Fatten them up before shipping them on to Chicago. I'd pay you a good salary, and you could even take a piece of the action yourself. Invest that money of yours and watch it grow. What do you say?"

Sounded good to me. I had money, all right, but I wasn't one to lay around and just spend it. So I'd said yes that day on the train, and we'd worked together for almost a year. Though Charley was a city man and almost twice my age, we'd got along real well.

Things were picking up down by the stage. Two of the men had moved the passengers away from the stage and forced the lot of them to sit on the ground. Another began cutting loose on the stage teams, while the fourth watched from horseback.

As the two started back, I figured now was my chance. As soon as they'd gotten clear of the passengers, I raised that Henry rifle and shot the fourth bandit off his horse.

"Stand right where you are," I shouted to the others. "We are federal marshals, and we've got you surrounded. Ain't a chance for you less'n you throw down them guns. Quick, now! Just as soon take you back across a horse as to have you in one piece. What'll it be?" They were slow in complying.

Moving quickly to my right, I raised the Henry again and shot a leg out from under the bandit by the teams. He fell heavily, his shotgun discharging harmlessly into the air.

"Aw right, boys," I hollered. "Let's kill them others. I got no patience with a man who don't know when he's licked."

Well, sir, that sure enough helped 'em decide. The guns hit the dirt, and their arms were reaching for the sky. The one by the teams was inching his hand towards his shotgun, a few feet away. I snapped off a round in close to the offending hand, and he lost interest in a hurry.

"You two," I shouted. "Git down on your bellies, and you try your durndest to look plumb to China. If I see so much as an eye blink, you're dead meat!"

"You! The messenger, I mean. Come on down and git your shotgun! That's right! Now jest you stand there behind the two on the ground. Kill 'em if they move an inch!"

One of the passengers, a youngish man, had reached down and picked up a revolver dropped by one of the holdups. He glanced at the cylinder, making certain it was fully loaded with ball. By the way he held the gun, I figured he'd handled one once or twice.

"You!" I hollered. "You in the blue suit! Go ahead and gather up the rest of them guns. Pile 'em up there by that driver on the box."

Watching, I saw him thrust the six-gun behind his trouser band and stoop for another. Moving with alacrity, he soon had all the weapons collected and stowed in the front boot.

Only then did I move out of the trees, nudging the big rawboned bay I'd rented in Atchison. The bandit I'd hit in the leg was groaning and clutching his thigh.

"You've played hell," he muttered. "Thet bullet cut the vein or somethin'. I'm gonna bleed out at this rate."

"Should of thought of that afore you stuck up this here stage," I retorted. "Git that belt off and strap it tight above the bullet hole. We'll git around to helpin' you as soon as we taken care of the driver." I glanced at the rest of the passengers. One of them pointed towards the stage.

"My bag is there in the back," he said. "I'm not a real doctor, but I was a surgeon's assistant during the war. I mostly treat animals now."

"Good!" I replied. "Let's git that driver down from the box and see what we can do for him. You!" I pointed at the man who had collected the guns. "Mister Blue Suit! Give them a hand gittin' the old man down!"

Together they lifted down the driver and laid him gently on the ground. His seamed face was gray with pain, and a moan came from behind clenched teeth as they started to remove his vest and shirt.

The lady passenger got her two cent's worth in. "You've got all you can do," she said, "just making sure that these robbers can't do us more harm. Let the doctor and I tend to the wounded."

"By the way," she continued, "where are the rest of your federal marshals? We could use their help!"

I grinned. "Reckon I'm it, missy. Just me! All by my lone-self. Far as that goes," I went on, "I ain't really no kind of law officer. Just a public-spirited citizen that's on the side of law'n order. I sorta figgered that'd give me some kind of edge on these here *bandidos* if they believed I had 'em surrounded."

She smiled. "Whatever your reasons," she told me, "it seems to have been successful. Now go on and do whatever a 'public-spirited citizen' does to secure these men, and the good doctor and I will handle our part."

Well, that sounded pretty good to me! I turned 'round to the feller in the blue suit. "Give me a hand with these two candidates for the gallows," I asked. "Seems a shame to be nursin' them other two back to health. If'n I had my way, a nearby tree would be bearin' ripe fruit about now. Man has a gun in his hand and uses it to rob folks is no more'n an inch away from bein' a killer. He'll shoot if you give him any trouble."

I turned and pointed at the downed swing horse, lying in the tangle of harness. He was quiet now, but his head moved slowly up from an arched neck, his anguished eyes staring huge and frightened. Blood was spurting from an artery that pulsed in his throat.

"Man that'd shoot a poor, dumb critter for no good reason at all is no better'n a hydrophoby skunk," I growled. "And he'd oughta be treated like one."

As I spoke, the horse's head dropped, and he was gone. I turned around and surveyed the balance of the stage's passengers. Of the three remaining, one appeared to be a dude of some kind. He was wearing a funny sort of cap, with earflaps fastened up and bills in front and back. Reckoned he was plumb scared because he still had his hands high in the air!

"You there," I told him. "You can put your hands down." I had to laugh. Even now he was looking from one side to the other as if for corroboration. Then, self-consciously, he lowered his hands and thrust them into his coat pockets.

"Sorry," I told him. "I couldn't help laughin'. But I'm not blamin' you for bein' scared. Man isn't scared when a gun's pointin' at him ain't got good sense. Don't you feel bad about bein' smart. I don't reckon you can ride a horse, can you?" I looked at the other two.

One from his outfit was a gamblin' man, and the other I figgered to be a drummer. A satchel with what looked to be hardware samples was lying by his feet.

"Lou Winters," he volunteered. "I can stay on a horse, I guess, but that's about it. Why? We have the coach, but of course somebody'll have to drive it."

The gambler had retrieved a short gun; one taken off him when the holdups had searched the passengers. He glanced at the rear of the cylinder, making sure the caps were still in place, then slid it into a holster under his left arm. With a tug at his lapels, he straightened his coat.

"One of those pigs has my bankroll," he said. "If you've no objection, I'll just retrieve it. As to your question, I can ride anything on four legs."

With that, he strode over to the two bandits, who were on the ground, their faces pressed into the grass. One of them had a flour sack bulging with loot tucked under his belt.

As he stooped to take the sack, he deliberately trod down on an outstretched hand, grinding a boot heel viciously until the bandit screamed with the pain. "That is for tearing my trouser pocket," he almost whispered. "And this—this is to make certain you never hold another gun." Raising his booted foot, he stomped down hard on the bandit's hand. A scream of agony raised the hairs on the back of my neck, and the man fainted.

Me, I'd had just about enough! Lunging into the tormentor's back, I sent him sprawling to the ground. For a large man, he was nimble; I'd grant him that. Like a cat, he came to his feet, his right hand snaking towards that hideout in his armpit.

The hammer of my Henry made two loud clicks as it cocked, and I motioned toward him with the muzzle. "Hang 'em!" I told him. "Like I said, I'm all for that. But do it neat and simple. Hurtin' a man when he can't fight back, that's a coward's way."

Judging by the look on his face, he was having a rock-hard time controlling his temper, but he sure wasn't no fool. My Henry's muzzle must have looked big enough to roll in a walnut, and I had him dead to rights. As I watched, that black look disappeared, and he taken his hand from under the coat.

"I'm sorry," he told me. "It's just that I've always had a dislike for any man to put his hands to me. I seldom lose my temper, but this time—" He waved his hands, palms out. "Look," he said. "I'm sorry, and I apologize. Now what is it you want us to do?"

The dude in the funny cap picked that time to get his oar in. His voice sure enough sounded different! Had a sorta twangy wheeze in it, like he was talking through his nose.

"I believe that you were addressing me when you asked as to whether or not I could ride a horse. Am I not correct in this assumption?" His face was kinda red to begin with; as he talked, it flushed even redder.

"It may surprise you to learn that not only can I manage to *remain* on a horse, but I am considered an expert in those arts pertinent to the equine. In other words, yes, I can, although I've never sat one of those grotesque saddles that you Americans seem to prefer."

Well, sir! I taken another look at him after that speech. He appeared to be about my age, and he was pretty well filled out. Not fat, you understand, but hard muscle. My maw'd told me more'n once that clothes don't make the man, and my guess was that this feller knew how to take care of himself no matter how peculiar he dressed. Or talked, for that matter.

I taken the Henry off full cock and transferred it to my other hand. "Name's Rush McCowan," I told him. We exchanged handshakes, and his grip was solid and dry. No pressure, but the potential was there, and I felt hard callus on that palm.

"Thomas Brooke, Esquire," he replied. "As you might have suspected, I am British. Bit awkward, you know. I'm afraid I'm not accustomed to this sort of thing. The highwayman is rather archaic, don't you know, although we had scads of the buggers in my country some hundred or more years ago."

I smiled. "Happy to say, it ain't exactly an everyday occurence in these parts, either, Mister Brooke. These boys mebbe know something we don't as to what's bein' carried in that express box."

"Anyways," I went on, "we got us a dead horse wrapped up in all that riggin', and he has to be drug outta there. I reckon we can use one of them outlaws' horses to fill in on the swing. Chances are he ain't never been in harness, but stuck in the middle, he'll be less likely to cause trouble."

I turned to the gambler. "Show this feller why we need our saddles rigged with a horn. Tell him about takin' *dally welters** 'round that horn with the rope. Take Mister Winters and let him help you untangle that harness. Don't recollect you sayin' what your name was.

"I don't believe I did say," he retorted. "But just call me Rousseau. C'mon, Brooke. I'll show you what he wants us to do."

Blue suit had the man with the smashed hand on his feet now and was leading him over by the stage. I prodded up my one remaining bandit with the Henry's muzzle. "Let's us go on over and join the rest," I told him. "Then we'll figger out what we're gonna do with you and your friends."

One pocket of his long linen duster was hanging somewhat heavier than the other, so I stopped him. "Just stand right there and keep them hands high. Let's see what you have in that pocket."

With a curse, he turned his head and glared at me, but I don't let dirty looks bother me. I stuck the Henry's barrel up into his armpit and reached down into the sagging pocket with my left hand.

"Well! Will you lookee here!" What I held up in my hand was a pepperbox pistol. Double action, with a ring trigger, it held five .36-caliber balls in as many barrels. Deadly at close range, it was an ideal hideout gun.

I shook my head sadly. "Reckon you just ain't the man to be trusted, my friend. Why, no wonder you ain't got nothin' better to do than to be out here holdin' up us honest folks." I tucked the gun into my chap's pocket and motioned him over to the rear of the stage.

The feller that'd hired me in Leavenworth had given me a set of handcuffs just in case. Using them, I cuffed him to one of the back wheels. "Now just you set there and study a spell,"

---

*From the Spanish *de la vuelta*—to take a turn.

I told him. "Could be you won't hang, after all. Why, you may not be facin' more'n twenty years in the pen."

The man with the bad hand was sitting sullenly, his back against a front wheel, while Blue Suit stood over him with a gun in his fist. The shotgun guard was helping Rousseau and Winters untangle the harness. As I watched, they got it all off and tied ropes to the dead horse's hind legs. Rousseau sent the messenger up to hold the leaders in place while he and the Englishman climbed onto two of the bandits' horses.

Squire Brooke was no stranger to a horse. That was plain to see. He squirmed around a bit before settling down, but he looked pretty much at home up there. I noticed that his toe alone was in the stirrup, not shoved all the way in to the heel, like we were used to doing. Course, he had on low-heeled boots, and I reckoned it was safer that way.

Rousseau showed him how to take a couple turns around the saddle horn with the end of his rope, and he picked that up quick enough. A moment later, they slid that dead horse out of there slicker'n grease.

One of the remaining bandit horses was a husky black and of a size with the rest of the stage team. I pointed my bay towards him and dismounted, shoving the Henry back into the scabbard. Taken but a minute to strip the saddle off, and I let it drop to the ground.

I left on the bridle and led both horses around to where the black could be harnessed. Surprisingly, he stood there, docile enough, while the rigging was buckled on and let the boys hitch him into the span.

The doc was waving at me to come over there, so I climbed back up on the bay and rode around to the other side of the stage. Both old man Forney and the robber I'd shot off his horse were lying on a couple blankets. Forney had his eyes open, but he was some pale around the gills. The other feller was unconscious. The third leaned back against a wheel.

"Not much I can do for this man's hand," the doc told me. "It's badly crushed, and there are a lot of small bones that are broken. I've wrapped it as best I can, but it will require a real doctor to set it right. Even then, I doubt the hand will ever regain any dexterity."

"How about Forney?" I asked. "How bad is he hurt? Don't look like he'll be drivin' stage for a while."

He grimaced. "No! Not for quite a while! That bullet went right on through his shoulder; thank goodness for that. At least there's less chance of inflammation. No bone broken there, but a lot of muscle damage. It will heal, but we can count on it taking at least a month, or more."

"The other man. The one you knocked off his horse. He's badly wounded. Your bullet glanced off his breastbone, tore some cartilage, and penetrated into his left lung. The ball is still in there, and I don't have the skill to remove it."

Forney was stirring. "Prop me up," he muttered. "Want to talk to my niece."

The lady passenger was standing right next to me. Before I'd had time to realize what Forney had said, she was stooping and had her arm around the old man's shoulders. "Won't one of you give me a hand here," she asked. "Don't you have any manners at all?"

Blue Suit was down there on the blanket before you could say "spit"! He propped old Forney against his shoulder and started fussing with the blanket. Forney just looked at him for a spell and asked, "Who'n hell are you, mister? Can't a man have any privacy around here? I want to talk to Ada."

"That's all right, Uncle Frank," the girl told him. "The man's just trying to help. What is it you want to tell me?"

The old man's head swiveled around. "You'll hafta be the driver, girl. Ain't nobody else can handle these horses. A stage ain't like an old buckboard, you know. Takes hands to drive these teams. Hands that know what they're doin'."

"Now just a dern minute," I hollered. "Ain't no outfit I can't handle. Besides, she's just a girl. Ladies are great for some things, but that sure don't include drivin' a stagecoach! Why! Why! She can't weigh much more'n a hundred or so pounds! Listen here, you crazy old man, I'm gonna be the driver of this here stage. Ain't never drove one before, at least not lately, but I'm gonna drive this one!"

The girl looked up at me and smiled sweetly. "Why, I'd never dream of doing something unladylike, Mister Whatever-I-should-call-you. But I've been handling the lines on these six-ups since I was a little girl. It doesn't take lots of strength, but it does take brains and a feel for the reins. By the way, who are you, and how did you just *happen* along?"

"Name's McCowan," I told her. "Rush McCowan. I was hired to trail along behind this stage and make sure it wasn't stopped by Injuns'n such. Feller in Leavenworth, representing the new owners, he's the one who hired me. So you see, I'm in charge of this here coach! I'm the one who picks out the

driver now that old Forney's hurt. Just because you're the old
man's niece don't give you no say-so around here!"

She was still smiling. "And who are the new owners? I
wonder if you even know their names."

"I sure do," I retorted. "McAlister's runnin' this line. He
bought it off of Wells, Fargo when they figgered it to be a
losin' proposition for a big outfit like them. Hell! The line only
runs from Atchison to Fort Kearny. That can't add up to more'n
250 miles or so."

"It's 253 miles," she told me. "And I am Ada McAlister!"
She was on her feet now, glaring up at me with fire in her
eyes. "That's right!" she said. "*I* am McAlister. That means
you're working for *me*!

"Now don't think for a minute that I'm not grateful. If you
hadn't been along, we'd be close to losing this line; at least
losing a reputation for dependability. I'm aware that you've
more than earned your money, believe me. But *I* will drive the
coach! I started with six pieces of line tied to fence stakes when
I was just a little girl and learned how to control six individual
horses harnessed together. They *are* individuals, you know.
Six of them, each one with ideas of their own as to where and
when to make a turn."

"Yeah! But I'm still—"

"Yes, I know," she came back. "You're a big, strong man,
and you're used to doing things your way. That's fine! But
you've never driven a coach. Wait, now, let me finish.

"I'm sure that you, like most others, realize that handling
a six-horse team is not the easiest job in the world. I will go
one step further. Imagine, if you can, what would happen to
this coach if all six horses turned at the exact same time. The
teams would be hopelessly entangled, and the stage would
overrun them, overturning in the process. Many, if not all of
them, would be injured, some with broken legs. We'd be lucky
if none of the passengers were killed.

"A turn has to be approached with anticipation. First, a
gentle pressure on the leader's rein and just a touch brake
pressure. Then, gradually, as the swings and wheelers reach
the turn, a tightening of all three reins on that side. We make
the turn much as a column of soldiers would execute the order
'column right' or 'column left.' With precision! I have the
experience, so I will drive the stage. Not because I am part
owner of the company, but rather because I know my business!
Now! Do you still have any objections?"

Now my maw never raised no foolish children. Nor one who didn't realize when he was dead in the wrong. What could I say against this lady when it was plain she knew more'n any of us when it came to driving a stage. I reached up, taken off my hat, and tried to keep a smile in my voice as best I could.

"You win, missy," I told her. "I'd appreciate it if you would be so kind as to drive this here stage. It might just be that some decisions will have to be made as to how and when we handle the rest of the trip. When it comes to that part of it, maybe you'll let me give you some advice. First off, we'd best decide which way we're gonna go. Do we go on back to Atchison so's a real doctor can treat the ones that are hurt, or do we keep on headin' towards Fort Kearny?"

Soon's I'd made my little speech, about a half a dozen of the others all tried to talk at once.

"I'm due in San Francisco no later than . . ." That was the feller in the blue suit.

"I have to be in Cheyenne by . . ." Rousseau's face was red, and he looked mighty angry.

"Makes no difference to me. I'd just as soon go back . . ." That was the drummer, Winters, his voice thin and reedy.

"We gotta go back, else I'm gonna bleed to death . . ." came from the bandit that I'd shot in the leg.

"How far is it either way?" asked the Britisher.

I looked down at Ada McAlister, and she was wearing somewhat of a frown on her face.

"Mr. McCowan! Would it be too much trouble for you to be down here on the ground with the rest of us? I'm getting a crick in my neck trying to carry on a conversation, and you insist on staying up there on that horse!"

"No! I mean, yes, ma'am! Why, I'm purely sorry, ma'am. I had no idea I was puttin' you to no inconvenience, ma'am! Anyways, I have me a list here of all the relays twixt Atchison and Fort Kearny and the distances between. We've just crossed into Nebraska 'bout a half hour back, and Otoe is the next station." I climbed down off the bay.

Flipping open a small tally book I'd taken from a pocket of my shirt, I glanced around. "Right now," I said, "the choice is like six of one and a half dozen of the other. I figger we'd best keep on towards Fort Kearny. It's further by about fifty miles, but there'll be better doctors at that fort than we'll find at Atchison. If we taken the stage on back, we're lookin' at a hundred miles or so. From here to Fort Kearny is about a hundred and fifty.

"We got Otoe comin' up next, and beyond that, Pawnee. At both of them, we'll just find fresh teams. They're only relays, or swing stations. Next will be Grayson's, and there we'll have hot grub, fresh horses, and a chance to rest up a spell. Grayson's is about thirty miles from here."

Winters waved a hand at me. "Will we be staying there, sleeping over, like we did at Laramie Creek last night?"

"Well, sir," I replied, "that's one of the things we'll be decidin' right now. My own self, I'd just as soon drive the stage straight on through to the fort. I figger we can make it in less'n thirty hours. Means little or no sleep, but we can git help for them that's hurt, and those of you with the tight schedules will be on time. Let's put it this way. I figger we'd best drive on through whether we go north or on back to Atchison." I motioned to Ada McAlister.

"You have an obligation," I told her. "I hope you remember that! You know! The government mail subsidy. If you don't stay on schedule, you'll lose the government contract, and I figger that pays some of the bills."

It was that old man, Frank Forney, who made up our minds. "We're goin' on to the fort," he cried out. "I'm hurt just about as bad as any, but I'll take my chances on the doctors we'll find at Kearny. Besides, that li'l bit of difference, fifty miles, don't amount to a hill of beans. Git goin'!"

"Well," I said, "that's settled. Now let's git the men that're bad hurt into the stage. That includes the two bandits. The one with the bad hand can ride on a horse. We'll tie his mount, and the one with the other badman, on lariats behind the stage. Squire Brooke can stay on his horse, ridin' alongside me. We'll foller some distance back."

CHAPTER 2

WHILE FORNEY AND THE BADLY WOUNDED BAN-
dit were lifted into the stage, I rummaged through the front
boot for a weapon that Brooke could carry. The rifle belonging
to the man I'd shot off the horse was a cut-down Springfield
conversion of a war-time musket. Originally a .58-caliber front
loader, it now had a hinged breechblock, and the barrel was
lined for a .50-caliber, center-fire cartridge. Someone had
chopped that barrel down to some twenty inches, and the stock
was cut off at carbine length. A piece of rawhide thong was
rigged into the trigger guard so's the piece could be hung from
a saddle horn. A sack of loaded cartridges was there with it.

Among the half-dozen handguns, I found a pair of .44-
caliber Remingtons, just like the one I was carrying on my hip.
One I taken out of the holster and stuck down inside of my
waistband. The other I gave to the squire, along with spare
packets of paper cartridges. These were in a large leather bag
attached to one of the holster rigs. The packages were water-
proofed with lacquer, and each held six loads, made out of
thin paper tubes, containing a powder charge and conical bullet.
These were marked JOHNSTON & DOW, and had been made in
New York. I stuffed a half dozen in my shirt pocket and let
Brooke keep the rest.

"By the Lord Harry," he said as he strapped on the holstered
revolver and hung the Springfield over the horn. "It takes me
back to my days in India. I was a subaltern in Her Majesty's
Sixtieth Rifles. Just a youngster, don't you know. I believe I
was only sixteen. It's been eleven years now. A riot was brew-
ing then. The native troops had been issued an Enfield rifle
that was to be loaded with a greased combustible cartridge.
Seems some blighter passed the word around that the grease
was from pig fat. You know, of course, that the *wogs* couldn't

13

touch any part of a pig. Strictly against their religion, don't
you know!

"Well! In order to load the rifle, one must bite off the end
of the packet, pour the powder down the bore, and ram in the
ball. The paper acted as a wad.

"Naturally, those buggers weren't about to allow pork fat
in their mouths. Meant they'd never go to heaven, or wherever
they expected to spend eternity. My word! It was riot and
mutiny wherever one would go! Junior officers and the ser-
geants were prime targets by their own men. They had to use
knives, of course. Those devilish curved ones, with an edge
so sharp, one could shave. I must say, we had a rotten time
with them before it was all settled!"

I doubt anyone else heard Brooke's little tale. I wasn't
surprised to hear that he'd seen combat. When we'd exchanged
handshakes, I'd figgered him to be a capable man. Seemed a
mite more cautious than most, but that didn't make him any
less of a man.

The bay was fidgeting, stamping his feet, like mebbe he'd
like to get to running. I taken a look around and figgered
everybody was about ready to shove off. The wounded were
in the coach along with the doc and Lou Winters. That feller
I'd been calling Blue Suit was standing by the door with Rousseau, trying to make up his mind where he'd ride. Walking
the bay over that way, I reached down and tapped him on the
shoulder.

"Reckon I know everybody's name but your's," I told him.
"Way it looks, we're gonna spend some time together, so we'd
just as well git introduced. What do fellers call you when they'd
like to git your attention?"

He sorta stared at the hand I'd offered. "Chilton," he told
me. "Captain Benjamin Chilton." He ignored my hand.

"Well, Captain Chilton, I wonder if you'd mind ridin' in
the stagecoach. These so-called roads are sorta bumpy, so's
we should have somebody hangin' on to the wounded men.
Mebbe you can trade off later on and git you some fresh air."
I turned away and called out to the others.

"Miss McAlister will drive, and the messenger will remain
up in the box. Rousseau! I'd like you to take the robber's
shotgun and ride up behind the driver. No tellin'! We can run
into more trouble before we git where we're goin'!" He picked
up the gun and clambered up on the stage roof without any
argument.

I watched Ada McAlister as she settled back in the seat, a
calm smile of assurance on her face. She unwrapped all of
them six lines from around the brake handle and taken them
confidently in her two hands. Carefully, she laid three of the
reins between the fingers of each hand, with the whip in the
curve of her right thumb.

"Heeyy yaaah!" she cried out as she kicked the brake out
of lock. I swear! Them horses acted like she'd been riding
along behind them since day one! They lunged into them old
breast straps like a fire'd been lit behind 'em, and we were off
and rolling.

For the next coupla hours, everything went along slick as
could be, with Brooke and me tagging along behind the would-
be stage robbers. The uninjured one had his wrists lashed onto
the saddle horn, and both were hobbled with a line running on
under each horse's belly. For a while, them horses fought a
losing battle against the ropes, holding them to the back of the
stage. The dust rolled up pretty thick back there, making it
darned uncomfortable and hard to catch a decent gulp of air.
Couple times I thought about stopping the stage so them bandits
could have a neckerchief pulled over their nose and mouth, but
then I got to thinking about poor old Forney and that hole in
his shoulder.

Brooke and I were far enough back and able to ride off a
bit to the side. We kept up a steady lope, with him keeping
an eye out to the east and me watching the other way. Then
we splashed across a shallow creek, and I saw a building, or
some sort of shack, ahead.

Otoe was just a soddy with a large pole corral attached. As
we came thundering down on it, I seen the stock tender run
out and stare, his arms waving in some sort of signal. The
corral was empty of horses.

In the doorway, I could see what appeared to be an Indian
woman, a child in her arms. She looked pretty scared!

I spurred my bay up close to where the bearded tender was
standing. "Where's all the horses," I hollered. Ada pulled the
stage in behind me and skidded to a stop.

"Injuns took 'em," he blurted out. "Come in here just about
daybreak. Warn't no use me tryin' to stop 'em. Popped caps
at 'em. Didn't even come clos' to 'em. There was one, had
him a long rifle. He shot me, here, in the head." He touched a
bloody bandage. "Thought he had me for sure, but it was jist
a graze. Old woman wrapped a rag around it. Stopped the

bleedin', but it shore hurts! Head feels like I bin hit with a
axe! Dunno, mebbe I never should've shot at 'em. Can you
take us along, mister? Them Injuns'll be back."

I doubted that. Didn't seem like there was anything left for
them to steal. This feller was wearing rags almost, or close to
it, and his woman looked almost as bad. The thieving Indians
had already taken the only things of value. The old shotgun he
clutched in his left hand was a wreck, with one nipple broken.
He could only use the left barrel.

"Not much range with that shotgun," I told him. "I doubt
any pellets even came close. Why ain't you got a rifle? If you
had something with some range to it, you might have kept them
Injuns from gitting our horses."

"Cain't afford it," he whined. "This job don't pay me no
money to speak of." He clutched at my sleeve. "You din't
come in here to pay me, did you?" He looked up hopefully.
"I ain't got no pay for four months now. They bin droppin'
off grub now and then. Stages brung me s'pplies 'bout three
weeks back, but I ain't see'd no money!"

I shook my head. "You're workin' for a new boss now. I
promise you'll git paid, and soon. Right now I can fix you up
with a decent rifle and plenty of cartridges. You wait. I'll be
right back."

There were two other rifles up in the boot. Both were in
good shape, having belonged to the bandits. One of them was
a Triplett Scott. They were a well-made gun; a seven-shot
repeater, chambered for .50 rim-fire but a mite complicated.
Mebbe too much so for the stock tender, who didn't seem to
be very bright. Operating its action required training.

The other piece was a Burnside carbine. Nice thing about
it was that it could be fired with both cartridge or with powder
and ball. I found twenty-eight cartridges in a pouch along with
a flask of DuPont's FFG and cast bullets in .54 caliber. Not
much he could do to harm the Burnside. It was a ruggedly
made weapon and shot dead on at about two hundred yards.
I'd fired 'em during the late war.

Ada looked over at me as I pawed through the pile. "Are
we still going to continue on to Fort Kearny?" she asked.

For some reason, that made me feel pretty good. She hadn't
been all that anxious to ask advice up to now. We'd gotten off
to a bad start, so to speak, and I'd figgered I'd come out on
the short end of the stick.

I studied her for a moment. She sure had beautiful eyes!

Right now they were sorta tinted with violet, and her long, dark lashes reached almost to her lower lids. Back there in the cottonwoods, when she'd been so mad at me, I'd sworn her eyes were coal black. Maybe they were when she was angry.

"We might's well keep on the way we're headin'," I said. "Even if they hit Pawnee Station and taken the stock, we're closer to Grayson's than if we went back to Laramie Creek.

"Think about it," I went on. "The teams we changed back at the last two stations were wore down when we left them. They ain't no better'n what we got right now. Accordin' to my tally book, we're twenty-five miles from Grayson's. That there's a home station, with hot grub *and* fresh horses. We can be fairly sure it'll be safe 'cause they got enough men there to stand off anythin' but a big party of Injuns. Just take it easy on these here horses we got, and if push comes to shove, we'll swap for some of these we're ridin'. Do you s'pose holdin' 'em down to an easy trot would help? Mebbe a stop now and then so's they git a chance to blow without a danger of stiffenin' up."

I reached out, cautious like, and touched her hand. "You just keep on doin' a good job with your drivin' and you can bet hard Yankee money that we'll come through just fine!"

She smiled, but it was a tight smile. "Whatever I said to you back there in the grove, consider it doubled. We're in your debt, all of us. It's easy to see that you've had a lot of experience being on the short side."

I noticed she wasn't making no effort to take her hand away, and I started to say something my own self.

"Well, mate, if you and the lady are done with the lolly-gagging, maybe you've time to listen to someone else. First off, I'm ready to trade my post in the stage. If you'll get me some line, I'll lash these men to the seats so that they can ride safe and secured. And," he added, "we won't be so busy hold-ing them that we can't hang on to ourselves."

Wouldn't you know. It was old Blue Suit again. Not that he was old, of course. I'd pegged him to be just about the same age as me, but he sure had a habit of turning up at the durndest times!

Right now he was grinning up at me, like he knowed I was none too happy about being interrupted. Ada had moved some, and her hands were in her lap. That durn messenger had sort of a sly look about him, also, and I reckoned he'd been listening

to every word we'd said and knew what I'd been leading up
to saying. First time I'd had Ada's attention.

Disgusted, I stepped down off the wheel, the Burnside and
ammunition in one hand. "You might's well git down off'n
the box and stretch your legs," I told him. Then, louder, with
authority in my tone, I called out again. "Let's everybody git
out here and walk around a bit." I turned to Chilton.

"The stock tender should have some soft cotton rope. The
kind he uses for team leads. That'd be better'n these grass
lariats we're carryin'. More comfortable, anyways. I have to
explain to him how this here carbine loads, so I'll ask. Mean-
times, I'd like you and Winters to break loose one team at a
time and water 'em there at the tank. Now don't, for gosh
sakes, let 'em drink a whole lot. Just enough so they can git
by 'til the next stop."

"Squire!" I called out. "Take this here bay of mine and
water him, along with your's. Not too much, you understand.
Just enough to wet their whistles. Better loosen your cinch a
mite. Give your horse a chance to breathe."

He looked at me with a trace of reproach. "Don't forget,
old fellow, I told you I was not lacking in experience. This
was common practice when we were following hounds."

Throwing an order at Chilton apparently had been a mistake
on my part. Right now he had something to say.

"What's the stock tender for?" he asked me. "Why should
I be doing his job? Winters and I are paying passengers, with
no agreement made about helping with the horses."

From the looks of him, I don't believe Captain Chilton ever
had been a lazy man. He was too husky to have laid around
while others did the work. Right then, I reckoned, he wasn't
in the mood to be bossed around, especially by me.

"You're righter'n rain," I told him. "But just now that feller
is scared half outta his wits and itchin' to ride on away from
here. Sooo... Would you *please* bear a hand so's we can
remove the temptation. I'd be most appreciative, and I apologize if that sounded like an order."

I was really right about the ragged man, who looked as if
he might bolt any moment. His Indian wife had moved closer
and was now huddled in behind him, the child clutched in her
arms. They were lucky, I mused. For some reason, the Injun
raiders had been content with stealing the horses.

The soddy looked like it could withstand a siege if they had
enough warning. The walls were at least two feet thick, and

the roof was more sod, with grass growing knee high. If attackers could get in close, I doubted the house would burn down. There were no windows in the back, and I mentioned it to the man when I taken him the carbine.

"Here's you a fine rifle," I told him. "And enough ammunition to stand off an army. First off, I'll show you how a cartridge is loaded, then how you can use loose powder with a cast bullet. First a warning. Be a good idea to make you a firin' slit in the back wall of your cabin. Right now it would be easy to git in behind, and you'd have no way to hit 'em before they fired the house. Not that it'd burn, cep'n for the roof grass, but it could git mighty hot in there!"

I showed him how working the lever would tip the breechblock back and down, allowing a cartridge to be placed rearward into the chamber of the block. "Now, when you bring it back up, the bullet part of the cartridge goes into the rear of the barrel, and that flange on the cartridge forms a seal against escapin' gases." I was demonstrating as I spoke.

"Next, you put a cap on the nipple and bring your hammer back to full cock. It's all ready to fire. With the battle sight, it will shoot right on at two hundred yards, so don't hold up high just 'cause your target's out a far piece.

"To shoot this here gun with loose powder, hang on to one of these cartridges. You'll need it for the seal, or you'll have a faceful of powder grains. Work the lever, put in the spent shell, and pour you a good charge of powder. Set that cast bullet down into it and close the breech. Then shoot it, the same's you did before." I looked around.

"Don't nobody git scared," I hollered. "I'm gonna demonstrate this here rifle."

About two hundred yards off, I saw a waist-high burl on a cottonwood tree where a limb had been broken off. Sighting right in the center of the burl, I touched off the Burnside. With that short barrel, it made quite a boom; a dirty-white cloud of smoke mushroomed from the muzzle, and the burl exploded!

Levering open the breech, I taken out the fired shell. A big grin on the stock tender's face showed his delight, so I handed him the gun. "Now just slip that shell back in and pour you a charge outta the flask. That's right. Next, the bullet, and close the action. Fine! Now, put a cap on that nipple and bring her back to full cock. Try a shot over in that same tree. Aim right where you want her to go!"

Surprisingly, he hit right in the same place I had, with fewer splinters flying but nevertheless a good shot. Turning around, he levered open the action and put the empty in his shirt pocket.

"Say!" he said, beaming. "That's some gun! I purely do want to thank you, mister. Like you said, I kin hold off an army!"

When I asked him about borrowing some cotton rope, he ran off to the soddy and brought back a coil. By then, Ada had joined me and had spoken to the Indian girl. She confirmed what I had told him about his pay.

"I'm going to deduct some," she said. "If you'll tell me what sizes you need, I'll see that the driver brings you out some clothing. Your wife has already said she'd like me to send along a bolt of gingham. Is there anything else you'd be needing?"

He bobbed his head. "No, ma'am," he replied. "Now that I got this here rifle gun, I got me no worries a'tall. And we shore do thank you, ma'am. Don't you fret none. Next time, ain't no Injuns gonna steal no horses around here!"

Looking back, I saw that the teams had been hitched, both bandits were in place behind the stage, and Chilton had gotten up on top with Rousseau. I warned the stock tender about being alert and said we'd see him later. Why, I don't know, since this had started out as a one-time job for me.

Brooke walked my bay over, and I stepped into the saddle, feeling it shift under my weight. Hastily, I slid back onto the ground and heard the squire chuckle.

"I say, McCowan. Wouldn't it be a good idea to draw that cinch tight before we ride off."

My face red, I did just that, muttering something about a bunch of greenhorns and me having to look after 'em.

With the cinch drawn up, I mounted again and rode closer to the stage. Handing Chilton the coil of rope, I grinned.

"Might not be such a bad idea to tie them fellers down to the seats, like you said," I told him. "Then you can ride wherever you dern well please. But—" I paused for a moment. "Keep that there pistol handy. Never know what's just around the next bend in the road."

I looked up at Ada, who'd already taken up the lines. "I reckon I'll ride on ahead a ways," I told her. "See what we got waitin' for us at Pawnee. You take care now, you hear? Them horses'll last if we just take it easy on 'em."

CHAPTER 3

I SPOTTED BAREFOOT PONY TRACKS ALONG WITH some from shod horses soon's I cleared the wagon yard. They headed in the direction of Pawnee Station, and more'n likely that meant we could forget about relief teams. My eyes picked out a faint blood sign mixed in, so there was a possibility that one of the stock tender's shots had notched meat.

About three miles further up the trail, the bay started a deep, rumbling whicker, and his ears shot forward. I pulled him up and slid the Henry out of its scabbard. The acrid, unmistakable smell of powder smoke hung in the air. Only a faint trace, but my oversized nose was seldom wrong. Ahead was a clump of willows with a few tall cottonwoods, and the strip of green extending out to both sides meant a creek. I touched spurs to the bay, and we walked slowly towards those trees.

Some fifty feet from the clump, I slid off the horse and walked alongside, keeping the bay between me and whatever I might find waiting in those trees. It was almighty quiet, I thought to myself. No bird sound—nothing! Just the scuffle of my horse's feet in the short grass and a faint plop as he planted a hoof.

Just inside that grove, I taken a wrap around a tree with the reins, leaving an end dangling in a slip knot. Might be I'd be wanting to leave in a hurry.

Cautiously, I moved on, the Henry held ready and cocked. The creek was barely ankle deep and moved sluggishly, without a sound. Just then, I heard the bare whisper of a moan.

Four more steps and I came out into a clearing. A naked man, his head raw and bloody, was lying there on the ground, remnants of clothing scattered around. Directly in front of me! His arms and legs were twitching, and I could tell that he was still breathing, so it wasn't just some reflexes. In that brief moment, sickened by what had been done to the man, I paused and closed my eyes. He'd been carved on, and bad!

Stepping around him, I catfooted across the clearing. Up against a cottonwood, I found another body. This one had no signs of mutilation and was still fully clothed. He was an older man. I'd say he was in his late fifties. A knife was still clutched in his left hand, and the blade was bloodied. Powder stains mingled with beard on the side of his face, an indication he'd been firing a rifle a heap of times, and his mouth was stretched out in a grim smile. A lance was driven through his chest, just below the breastbone. One leg had a bloody hole above the knee, and it was twisted at an unnatural angle.

Sign was easy to read. This one had held out right to the last. Chances are he'd have used his teeth on them if he could have gotten close enough. Waugh! Crippled up and surrounded by his enemies, he'd held out to the last, slashing them with his knife when they got in close. Bravery is a special thing with Injuns. They'd respected this man, and that's why he still had his hair.

A sound from the other poor devil turned me around, and I knelt down by him. But it was just a dying breath. He died with his mouth open and his eyes staring with fright. Hard to find any fault with his apparent cowardice. Who knows if he will be brave until that time comes. I stood up, and my thoughts were not happy ones. Maybe, in some faraway town, a widow or mother might grieve for a loved one. A son or a husband who was long overdue. But they'd never know how or where that loved one had passed away.

Wasn't much I could do about burying them. I had no time to dig graves even if I'd had a shovel. I could tell someone at Pawnee Station or Grayson's, and they could come out with the proper tools. Circling through the trees, I stumbled into a dead pony lying half into the creek. One of his eyes was just a bloody hole, and a rusty stain ran down that side of his neck. Looking more closely, I could see the end of a large rusty nail protruding from the eye socket. That stock tender must have used whatever was close at hand for a shotgun charge.

From the sign, I figgered the Indians had been gone for a good three hours. The tracks led off toward Pawnee Station, about eight miles up the stage road. Jerking loose my reins, I stepped into the saddle and shook out my rope. It wasn't like Injuns to leave a dead critter in a watering place, but I could do something about it no matter the reason. I tied onto that

pony with my rope and drug him out onto the bank, far enough
off there'd be no danger of poisoning the water.

Touching my hat brim to the man by the tree, I rode on off,
coiling the lariat and strapping it back to the pommel. My
thoughts went back to the stage and Ada, sitting high up on
that box, coaxing those horses along. She sure enough had a
fair share of pure grit! Hopefully, she'd pass by the grove
without stopping to water the teams.

I kicked the bay into a lope and kept an eye out for any
sign of dust or anything that might indicate I was closing. By
the sun's angle, it was coming on four o'clock, and those folks
behind me might just be feeling hungry. I was, and my small
supply of *carne seca*, or jerked beef, had been used up the
night before, when I camped out close to the stage stop. Before
this day was over, I might be wishing I'd carved me a couple
of big steaks off of that dead Injun pony. If we had another
raided swing station waiting for us at Pawnee, not a spare team
to be had, then it'd be late into the night when we pulled into
Grayson's Station.

From the trail sign, I picked out at least twenty horses with
shod feet. Could be some of the Indians were riding on part
of them, but it was hard to tell with the ground so dry and
powdery. The unshod ponys numbered another fifteen, but they
could be shifting from horse to horse. Best I figgered out was
that we were faced with mebbe sixteen or more Injun warriors,
and that was enough to make a man think about it.

I could count on the squire up to a point. A man that'd
shoot all day at game might think twice before he killed a
fellow human. Rousseau! No problem! He'd kill without any
hesitation. Chilton, too, once he got the first shot off. I figgered
the shotgun messenger would have no doubts. It was his job!
What was his name? Sam! That was it! Doc Talbot would shoot
at 'em, but more'n likely take no aim. And Ada! From what
I'd seen so far, she'd do what had to be done. My real doubts
were with Lou Winters, but I could be dead wrong about him.
Some fellers fool you. Under stress, they might turn out to be
hell on wheels.

Sooo . . . I had three or four I could count on in a fight, if
it came to that, and another three that would at least be firing
in the general direction of our attackers.

I got down off the bay and walked for a spell. He was a
good, solid horse. No prize winner when it came to looking
handsome, he was a real stayer. I found myself wishing that

my saddlebags held some grain for him. Horse can't keep on going strong without he has something besides plain grass.

Then I saw the smoke. We still had some four miles or so to go before we reached Pawnee, but I had no doubts that smoke was coming from there.

I climbed back onto the bay and kicked him into a run, a hard run that we couldn't keep up for long. For some reason, I wanted to see—actually see—those damn Injuns. Don't ask my why 'cause I'd have no answer for that. It was a stupid thing to do, but I did it, anyways.

Inside of two miles, he was breathing hard. Another half mile and I had to bring him down to a walk. His breath was coming hoarse, and his sides moving out'n in like a bellows. I jumped off and ran alongside the horse, my Henry ready in one hand and the reins in the other.

We splashed across two creeks, running side by side, sometimes stumbling and falling against each other. Then down into a shallow gully and up the other side. My lungs burned, and I could feel a sharp pain in my side.

Topping out on a slight rise, I looked down on all that I figgered was left of Pawnee Station. A long, squat building blazing away, with a couple of smaller structures also burning. A big horse corral with the gate wide open and stock nowhere in sight. A dust cloud, several miles beyond, showed up against the horizon. There went my Injuns. The ones I'd been so anxious to see up close!

The bay was stumbling, and his head hung down. I reached over, loosening the cinch, and I taken my canteen off of the saddle horn. Pouring water over my neckerchief, I carefully sponged out the horse's mouth and nostrils, then poured some over his head. Taken a swallow myself and rinsed my mouth. Didn't dare let the bay stand or he'd stiffen up, so I patted him a time or two, told him what a fine horse he'd turned out to be, and led him on down the slope.

Pawnee Station had been a pretty nice layout. The buildings had been made from squared logs, with neatly dovetailed joints at the corners, and the windows had held glass. Near the front door, I saw a well-made workbench, with a partially completed cabinet lying on one side, the flower beds that showed careful tending were along the front footings.

The bodies of two men were sprawled near the corral gate, both badly hacked and mutilated. More'n likely, they'd been about to harness up the teams for the incoming stage.

I'd just about had my fill of dead bodies. Sickened by all the needless slaughter, I led the bay around to a large wooden water trough just inside the corral. There, crumpled in a bloody heap, I saw the body of a young boy. Couldn't of been no more'n seven, eight years old. Like the others, he'd been scalped. The bay was just too plain tired to even shy. I stripped off the saddle and blanket and hung 'em over the corral rails. The blanket was wringing wet, and so was that poor horse's back.

I let him have a little water and taken him to one side where there was some straw piled up. Rubbed him down with a handful as best I could. I had to cool him out, or he'd be of no use to me, or mebbe even dead!

Then it occurred to me. Where there was a little boy, there might just be a mother! I hadn't seen another body in the wagon yard. Where? Where would she be?

Dragging the bay behind me, I trotted over near the front door of the main building. The heat from the fire was really intense, but there weren't any flames in the doorway itself. The horse would stay anchored; I was sure of that. I dropped the reins and plunged through the doorway. Lots of smoke inside. So much I had to get down next to the floor where there was some air to breathe.

Everything got in my way! Table and chairs—a stove. I got tangled up in a blanket that had been used to curtain a section of the one-room cabin, and I fought it off, cursing. I was about to give up when I reached into what appeared to be bedding and found my hands touching the soft contours of a woman's body. A moan, followed by a convulsive arching of her back, proved she was still alive, but just barely. Only torn rags remained of her clothing. She clutched at me and then fought me, muttering words I couldn't understand.

"It's gonna be all right!" I hollered. "I'm no Injun! I mean to git you'n me outta here if you'll give me a chance. Jest don't be scared, lady. I'm tryin' to help, honest!"

She pushed at me, but she was so weak. I taken both of her hands in one of mine and started crawling back. It was easier now because I could see daylight at the door. Dragging her across the floor, I ran the same obstacle course of table and chairs. I wished that I dared stand, but the heat was not as bad near the floor, and I could breathe. Then we were at the door, and I saw the stage swinging in. I stooped down and gathered the limp form in my arms. Staggering, I carried her out into the wagon yard, then fell headlong to the ground.

Ada was up there on the box, her eyes wide, a shocked look on her face. Then the door to the coach swung out, and Doc Talbot was running toward us, a black bag in his hand.

I raised up on an elbow and tried to grin, but it smarted some. I reckoned my face was burnt. I'd lost my hat in the scuffle and couldn't remember where. Then Doc was next to us, kneeling, a look of concern on his homely face.

"Don't bother with me," I told him. "Look after the lady there. She's been hurt pretty bad."

Talbot taken his coat off, wrapping it around the injured woman. I hunkered up and watched as he cradled her tenderly in his arms, trying to sponge away some of the blood. It was obvious that she was dying. Pushing at him, she mumbled something and made vague gestures toward the burning stage station. A grimace of pain contorted her features.

Then her chest swelled, her eyes widening as she came to an almost erect position in his arms. "Baby..." she whispered. "My baby... Cellar... In cellar... Baby..."

Her eyes rolled back, and she went limp in Talbot's arms. I heard a deep sigh, and she was gone. Doc laid her back gently on the ground. He looked over at me, his eyes moist with tears, and dabbed ineffectually at blood on his shirt.

"She's dead," he said brokenly. "Perhaps if I had more skill..." He looked down at that slight form lying quietly beside him. "Horrible!" He shuddered. "How? How could men do that to anyone, much less a woman? Savages! Inhuman and cruel savages! Such a terrible thing!"

"Wasn't much you could do," I told him. "She was already past help. They hurt her pretty bad. Right now we have to quick figger out what she meant by a baby in the cellar." I stood up and brushed at my pant leg. My holstered revolver had swung around and was dangling between my legs, so I swiveled it back into position on my hip.

"If there's a cellar," said Ada, "it would be there, beneath the floor of the station building. But it's too late for us to try. The roof could collapse at any moment."

To tell the truth, the last thing I wanted to do was run into that blazing fire. "I'll try," I told her. "If there's a trap in the floor, I reckon it'd be near where they cooked meals. Chances are it'll be a root cellar and a place for storin' food in airtights." I began to unbuckle my gun belt.

"The hell, you say!" It was good old Blue Suit again. I looked over at him and saw a grim smile on his face.

"I been in fires before," he told us. "Ship fires that presented more problems than we'll ever face here. It helps to know what you're doing and can keep your wits about you. Easy to get turned around, what with the smoke and all; then you're trapped, and you don't get nothing done. Don't worry none because I know what I'm doing. With that knowledge, I am taking a calculated risk, not pulling a damn fool stunt."

He shrugged out of his heavy coat. "Water," he told us. "I need water, and lots of it. Where do they keep it? That corral over there?" I nodded, and he taken off, running.

A moment later, he came back, the coat dripping wet, and I watched as he draped it over his head and shoulders. "Find some buckets," he told us. "Fill them with water and be in close with them. Douse us good when I come back out. Say! McCowan! Any idea where that galley area might be? Did you notice by any chance?" He was about to enter the building, and this last question had been hollered over his shoulder.

So much for his idea of a "planned risk," I mused grimly. He'd thought it out, all right, except for a very important and necessary bit of the "knowledge" he'd claimed would help. It was somehow comforting to know that Captain Chilton could be rattled in an emergency, same as us regular folks.

"Might try the wall to your far left," I shouted. "That's where I ran into the stove. You sure you want to do this?"

He nodded and turned away. Smoke was billowing out from the open doorway, but no flame showed as yet. Ducking down, he gathered the coat closer around him and ran through that dense cloud of smoke, disappearing instantly.

Winters, Rousseau, and the messenger joined us then, and between them they had five buckets of water. I glanced over toward the stage and saw the squire was guarding our prisoners, the Springfield cradled in his arms. He'd elected to stay on his horse, and they remained on theirs. Our wounded had been left unattended, but I figgered they'd be all right for a while. Better that Talbot stood by in case Blue Suit did find a child somewhere under that blazing inferno.

I motioned to the three men with buckets, and we formed a semicircle as close to the door as possible. Taken one of the buckets Winters was holding and had it ready. The heat of the fire was almost unbearable, and perspiration made the slight burns on my face really sting. It seemed Chilton had sure enough been in there for an awfully long time.

Then! There he was! Lurching through the doorway, a bun-

dle in his arms and the wetted coat over them, steaming. A
heel caught on the door sill, and he fell, sprawling, at our feet.
Fortunately, he was able to twist around so's to land on his
back, the bundle held out of harm's way. Five large buckets
of water hit him about then, and he sat up, sputtering.

Both Talbot and Ada reached for the bundle he held aloft,
but my lady boss was quicker. Hugging the blanketed form in
her arms, she hurried back to a safe distance from the fire,
with Doc right behind.

I started to follow, as did the others. "Avast there, my
overeager friend. I have something here for you." Chilton threw
off the sodden coat and pulled a flattened, shapeless bit of felt
from under his belt.

"Your hat, McCowan! I found your precious Texas hat you
prize so highly! Apparently, in your struggles with all the
furnishings in there, it came adrift. Here! Take it!" His grin
was a broad one as he held out the battered hat.

Not to be outdone, I grinned on back. "Why, can't tell you
how much I 'preciate this, cap'n. That there hat's sort of a
good-luck charm for me. I'd be feelin' mighty uncomfortable
without I had it." I reached out a hand, and he taken it, then
pulled himself to his feet.

"Yessirree, Bob! I'm mighty obliged, Cap'n Chilton! And
most grateful to you for riskin' your neck to save my lucky
sombrero. Why, when I consider how you even sac'ficed them
fine mustachios of yours, that surely taken months...." My
voice trailed off as he clapped a hand to his upper lip, on which
remained only a charred, curling stubble. All that he had left
of a blond handlebar mustache!

I had to give him credit. He started to say something, and
I'd venture to guess it would not have been intended for mixed
company. But he held it back, and would you believe it? He
actually smiled at me!

Now some folks might think I was talking mighty foolish
when you consider that we'd just watched a lady die and had
two men and a little boy lying out there, killed and scalped by
Injuns. But worry won't get the job done, and sometimes a
comical word or two will help folks perk up.

I figgered Chilton had been over the mountain and seen a
varmint or two; only mebbe, in his case, them mountains might
have been big waves. I reckoned he knew I was speaking fun
and knew why I was doing it.

"Let's git on over there and see what you've found, cap. Is it a boy or a little girl?"

"I'm damned if I know," he replied. "Whatever it is, we got a live one. Never hear one child make so much racket!" He glanced down at his dripping suit. "Let's make it quick so I can climb out of this wet uniform. I have a change if we can find my sea chest where they buried it in the boot."

He stuck out his hand. "My friends call me Ben, and I feel we should give it a try, don't you? You've done a real shipshape job so far. If I've shown any resentment at the orders you've given me, chalk it up to the fact that suddenly you were there! The stage was being robbed, and all of a sudden, you showed up to save the day!

"I'm not used to being helped, if you must know," he went on. "Normally, I get myself out of my own scrapes. I guess I was feeling rather helpless, and that made me mad! With a gun stuck up my nose, there wasn't much I *could* do. Believe me, I've had this tried before, and I've never let them get away with it. I maybe got a scratch or two, but I fought my way out. With the lady there, I didn't dare try anything!

"Wait a minute. Let me finish. What I'm trying to say is that I resented you bailing us out. Made me look like a fool, you see. Me, who has fought waterfront toughs in most of the ports of the world and never came out second best. I sailed before the mast when I was only twelve years old in ships of every nationality, and I asked no favors, believe me. Now I'm asking one of you. Let's start all over again."

He stuck out that hand again, and I taken it. There for a minute, I thought he was gonna put on the pressure, but he didn't. We shaken hands and went to see what he'd fetched.

CHAPTER 4

WE'D FOUND A COUPLE SHOVELS WHERE THE stock tenders had a hole dug for a new privy and given our dead a decent burial on a knoll back of the station. Ben's rescued bundle turned out to be a little girl about two years old. She'd cried a spell at first, but Ada's soothing words calmed her down in a few minutes. But she sure wanted her mama!

That old sun was getting mighty close to the horizon, and we had fourteen miles to go if we figgered to make the next station. I'd cooled my bay out by walking him for more'n a half hour, but he needed rest bad! Squire Brooke said that he wouldn't mind riding on top for a while so's I could use his horse. A big, leggy chestnut, he was in fine shape. We switched rigging and tossed the bandit's saddle on top. No telling, we might just need another saddle and bridle, and I hated to see anything go to waste.

Everybody got on board, and I taken a last look around. I warned Rousseau and the squire to watch the pair in back as I climbed onto the chestnut. "And keep your eyes peeled for Injuns," I cautioned them. "Just because I figgered they had long gone doesn't mean they didn't leave some behind."

Ada kicked off the brake and hollered at her leaders. A moment later, we were on our way. With luck, we'd be covering the fourteen miles in about two hours and pull in there an hour before dark. Ada had held her teams down and tried to keep 'em at a fast walk. This way, if we did run into an ambush, they'd still have a fast mile or so in 'em. If is a big word, as we all know, and I for one was keeping all my fingers crossed. I'd relax when we got there!

Ben was on the box between Ada and the messenger, and it seemed to me that they were almighty close together. Then I told myself to leave off that foolishness. Ada was a growed woman, and I had no call to be jealous. Far as that went, I was just her em-ploy-ee! She'd been nice enough to me. Who wouldn't after you'd saved their bacon? But never a bit of encouragement in any other way. No hint that she cared.

Whooo wheee! Rush McCowan, I chided myself. Not more'n a year ago, you figgered you had Julia all sewed up. Figgered all you had to do was to come home to Texas, a pocketful of money in your kick, and Julia'd fall all over you. And what happened? She married your brother Milo! Face it! You're big, and you're ugly, and ain't no woman gonna fall all over herself making up to you. Ada's grateful, but that's all!

I waved to her and the rest, then spurred that chestnut a tad and got him into a swinging lope. I'd explained to the others that a scout ahead made sense and planned to range a couple of miles in front of the stage. In the event that an Indian war party had hit Grayson's, I wanted to have lots of warning beforehand.

The sky to my left was turning a reddish orange, and that meant we could expect good weather tomorrow. It was getting on into September, and rain was not infrequent at this time of year.

The big, rangy gelding under me was really running proud! He kept his chest and head well up, and the powerful rhythm and reach of his stride was something to see. I've had fellers tell me that a horse is a dumb critter and can't even remember further back than his last good meal. Might be the truth with some, but I've owned horses that could do most of what humans could cep'n mebbe read'n write. Man riding the owl-hoot trail needed a strong, smart horse, and this one was all of that! I'd admired this animal even when I'd knocked his rider off with my Henry rifle.

As we loped along, my thoughts went back a year, to a day in August when we'd started our drive to Abilene. The hand riding right flank was a Mexican feller named Luis Marindo. Luis was on his favorite cutting horse that day, a chestnut gelding about the same size and conformation as this one of mine. Horse was after a bunch-quittin' steer, dodging about and swapping ends quicker'n the eye could follow. I'd said something to Luis. Told him the horse looked like he'd keep on going strong even if the job taken all day.

He'd grinned at me and said they had a sayin' in Mexico, *"Un caballo alasan tostado muerte antes que ser cansado."* A rough translation went: "A chestnut horse will die before he tires." I'd believed it then, and I was sure of it now! This old boy I was straddling was eager! His ears were both flicking back and forth, and he was plainly excited and interested in where we were going.

Thinking back to that day we'd started the herd outta the Val Verde got me to daydreaming. It was safe enough. This four-legged partner of mine would give me plenty of warning if we even got close to Injuns. In joshing myself about the lady boss's feeling toward me, I'd thought of myself as big and ugly. To tell the truth, I'm the smallest of three sons in my family.

Milo, who was two years younger'n me, was about three inches taller than my six-three and outweighed me by twenty pounds. Baby brother Lysander stood six-ten and tipped the scales at three hundred. Even my maw topped the six-foot mark.

Our paw, Ebit McCowan, had been gone now for eight years. A full-blood Choctaw Indian, his real name had been a tongue twister, *Ebita Poocola Chitto*, meaning Big Person, Source, or Fountainhead. Maw's name was Abigail McCowan, and when they married, he shortened his to plain Ebit Mc-Cowan.

We boys all had paw's fair-sized nose and naturally dark skin. Me! I'd turn black if I was in the sun for long. I been proud of that Injun blood all my life and tried really hard to live up to it. Injuns is just folks, just like everybody else. There's good ones, and there's some that're about the baddest you'll ever find anywhere. But that same streak is found in plenty whites.

Some fellers is just naturally ornery and ain't satisfied less'n they're hurting someone or some thing. You know the kind I mean. They're hard on horses and livestock. They ain't happier than when they're picking on a smaller man. In a fight, they'll always take the advantage, and some are just downright blood-thirsty! The bunch that had scalped a little boy and savaged his maw fit into that category. Course, a chief could be telling his warriors that what they had done was just repaying the whites for some mischief they'd cooked up and that they were in the right. The young men are more easily influenced, especially after they listen to all those war stories, and just can't wait to get out there where the coups are waiting to be counted.

I'd met a real Injun Chief, the year before. A feller named *Tené-angópte*, which meant Striking Eagle in Kiowa. He had no particular love for the whites, but he was smart and knew his people didn't stand a chance of whipping them. But when he tried to tell his folks that peace was the only way out, they didn't believe him. Called him a coward and even tried to kill him. He'd farmed two young Kiowa boys off on me, and they'd turned into first-class cowhands. Right now, I reckoned they were working on the CMC connected, our brand back in Texas.

Ahead, I could see a strip of green, with some cottonwood trees in a clump. Horse hadn't even raised a sweat, but the rider could stand a rest and mebbe a smoke.

I was carrying the Henry across the saddle bows and figgered I was ready for most anything that might turn up. The rifle was part of a swap I'd made down in the nations while we were making that drive last year. Little Raven, a chief of the Arapaho, threw it in on a trade for some sore-footed, lamed horses we had no further use for right then.

It was a beautiful piece, fully engraved on the action, a feller's name, Enoch Hand, in a banner on the right side. I had to file some on the firing pin because it had jammed in the bolt. Somebody had snapped it, repeatedly, without cartridges in the chamber. Not being able to fix it, the chief had placed no value on the gun. Me! I wouldn't sell it for a pocketful of money. Not now! It held fifteen rounds in a magazine under the barrel, and it shot right where I pointed it! That's all that mattered to me. I had me one of Winchester's new, short-barreled carbines that shot the same .44 rim-fire cartridge, but not to the long-range mark like this old gal. Some fellers carry lucky pieces. An old coin, the hind leg of a rabbit, mebbe a lock of a loved one's hair. I had me this Henry rifle, and she was all the luck I needed!

The green strip turned out to be a shallow creek. On the far side, I found tracks of at least a hundred unshod ponys. Saw where the sign I'd been following mixed in with this new batch of riders coming up from the south.

Stepping down, I ground-reined the chestnut and studied for a minute or two. Hard to tell who was who once all the tracks got together, but what was most important to us, that whole bunch had turned north! The stolen teams were held in the center, with barefoot tracks on all sides.

Seemed like the ones who'd raided the stations were mebbe just a small party from this larger one; and now they'd got back together, they'd head for home. Where that was, I sure couldn't

care less. Just so long as they kept off the stage road. Looked
to me like mebbe we'd make it, after all.

I got out my pouch and rolled a smoke. After I got that
fired up, I decided to prowl around a bit more. Food scraps
were littered on both banks, so I figgered they'd spent some
time in the grove. The creek was still cloudy from mud but
was beginning to clear. By the time the stage got this far, Ada
would be able to water her teams.

Grayson's was seven or eight miles further on. Might not
be a bad idea for me to hold up here for the stage and make
sure they read the sign right. About now, I imagined they'd
welcome a piece of good news for a change. While the teams
were being watered, I could go on ahead and scout the road.

Loosening the cinch, I let the chestnut take a little sip from
the creek where the water was running clear over rocks and
sand. Rolled me another smoke, then cinched up the saddle
again and moved the horse back onto some grass. Soon's I tied
the picket rope to a tree, I taken out on foot, heading south
down the far creek bank.

I found some shod horse tracks mixed in with those of the
Injun ponys, which could mean that the main party had made
a raid somewhere along their line of march. The marks were
of smaller size, not like those of draft horses. Probably they
had hit a ranch or two and run off the saddle stock.

A glitter of steel caught my eye, and I reached down and
picked up a knife with a broken blade. It had been crudely
made—probably pounded out of a wagon spring or a brace on
a double tree. The handle was wooden and had a buffalo head
realistically carved on the butt end. Probably big medicine to
whoever had owned the knife, and I wondered how it'd gotten
broken and why he had thrown it away. Almost looked as if
the break was deliberate. Mebbe some sort of sign, as if he'd
been disgusted or had given up. I stuck it down in my chap's
pocket. The Injuns here in Nebraska, and their ways, were
strange to me. Mebbe this knife would be a clue to who had
attacked the stations and done the killings.

After I'd scouted along the creek for a quarter mile, the
more I was convinced that I'd underestimated the size of the
war party. There were tracks crossing tracks, but the piles of
pony droppings in that quarter mile made it out to be an easy
two hundred riders, mebbe more.

Last I'd heard, most of the Sioux had gone on the dole a
good six months ago. Holed up on reservations the army had

set up for 'em. A day or two before I taken this job, I saw
where the Santee Sioux had sent all their kids to a class at the
reservation school in Niobrara and were farming potatoes and
corn. Read it in the Leavenworth *Daily Conservative* at the
National Hotel. Right on the front page, under the item about
U.S. Grant running for president against Seymour. The paper
didn't say anything about the rest of the Sioux, and I reckoned
there were lots more of 'em.

Crossing over the creek, I worked my way back towards
the picketed chestnut. Just as I came up on him, I saw his ears
shoot forward and heard the sounds of the stage coming in.

Ada and the rest were mighty relieved to hear that them
Injuns were heading north. She got that messenger down and
told him to unharness the teams, water 'em, and put them out
on pickets for a while. I'd already suggested that we spend a
half hour or so, giving them some rest. Ben Chilton taken that
Triplett & Scott rifle out of the front boot and asked me to
show him how it operated. Even though we'd decided to be
friends, I could see he was none too happy about asking.

"Pistols work just fine," he told me. "That is, if whatever
you're shooting at is no more than fifty feet away. A rifle's
the thing for this long-range work.

"Now I've already figured out how the cartridges load in
this tube, running up into the butt stock. How on earth do you
get them from there up to the chamber?" He handed over the
rifle, a look of frustration on his face.

"Like everything else, Ben, it's simple if you know how.
Look! See this here catch just behind the hammer? Push it
down, twist the barrel to the right, and you'll see that the
chamber lines up with the front end of the magazine tube." I
was demonstrating as I spoke.

"Let's say you just fired the rifle. Now you twist your barrel
and breech to the right. As you do this, a spring is throwing
out the fired case. The magazine cover's pushed to one side,
allowing one round to be fed from the magazine. A twist back,
cock the hammer, and she's ready to fire. Seven shots—that's
how many the magazine will hold. That's simple enough, isn't
it?

"By the way," I added. "Don't worry about that crack you
see in the stock. They all have it. Leastways, most all
I've ever seen are that way. It's because of the way it was
drilled for the tube. Won't hurt anything. It's plenty strong

enough unless you decide to use it on someone's hard head. I can't guarantee it won't break then."

He nodded and thanked me. Ada had disappeared, so I had Squire Brooke give me a hand with the two bandits we'd tied on horseback behind the stage. I figgered they must be the stiffest and most thirsty fellers in Nebraska about now. I reckon I could add "angry" to what I just said.

Neither could stand very well, and the one with the hand that was all smashed up was a pretty sick man. We got them down off the horses, and neither one could make it without a helping hand. I taken 'em by the arms and led them towards the creek, with Brooke following behind, leading the horses.

Once they'd drunk their fill, I sat 'em down on the bank and asked if they'd like a smoke. Both had the makings, but I had to roll a quirly for the one with the bad hand.

"You fellers got names?" I asked them as I passed around a lit match.

"What business is it of yours," one asked surlily. "You ain't no more U.S. marshal than we are. 'Nother thing, jest who'n hell you think you are, holdin' us prisoner like this? We got friends up the line that'll make you damned tough to ketch without you turn us loose, and right now!"

I nodded. "Me? I'm the feller that had me a chance to kill all of you deader'n stomped-on snakes. Why, the four of you are nothin' but a bunch of ama-choors! Back home, in Texas, we got us a twelve-year-old boy that'd chew you two-bit bad-men up and spit you out like buckshot! You do fine when it comes to wavin' guns at women and unarmed men, but I seen how fast you back down when the odds seem ag'in you.

"I could keep you for bait. Them Injuns git in close, we might jest hand you over to 'em so's we can git on our way. If we do, I won't have to worry about your friends, 'cause it might jest be they'll never know what happened to you. You study on that for a while.

"Now I don't exactly care whether you give me your real names or not. I ain't thinkin' about no re-ward, nor nothin' like that. If you want, I can call you by a number, but if'n I was you, I wouldn't like that on my tombstone. We're in a tight fix here. By the sign, them Injuns has gone and turned north, and mebbe we won't see 'em no more. But then we might jest be lookin' at the whole Sioux nation some'ers betwixt here and Fort Kearny. If we do, I may have to trust you fellers with guns; so I'd like to know who I'm gonna run down and skin out if you decide to leave for other parts."

The feller with the bad hand looked slantways at his buddy. "My name's Halloran," he said. "But they calls me the Cherry Creek Kid on account I come from Colorado. My sidekick here is Bowie Knott. Them other two; the ones you shot up back there . . . Right now, I reckon we'd best call 'em by any name as suits you. How about Smith and Jones?"

"That's right," said Knott. "Me'n the Kid'll make up our own minds, mister, but Smith and Jones it has to be until I hear them say dif'runt. By the way . . . How're them boys doin'? Is thet sawbones wu'th his salt?"

"Far's I know, they doin' all right," I told him. "But I reckon the feller I shot off the horse is hit hard, and that ball is still in his chest. Which one *is* he? Smith . . . ?"

Both of the men grinned, and Knott asked if I'd mind making him another smoke. "Whereabouts in Texas you from?" the Kid asked.

"Over close to the Big Bend," I told him. "East of Pecos Valley, in what we call the Val Verde. My maw'n my brothers are takin' care of our place right now. We got us some'ers around eight sections deeded land and plenty of water. The home place sits right above Beaver Lake, on Devil's River."

I lit the cigarette for Knott, and he nodded thanks. "I'm from Texas myself," he told me. "Born and raised on a farm near Maude. My pa wanted me to be a preacher. Can you feature thet? Sent me to the old Union School there. It cost him some money, too. Thet's what they call a 'subscription' school. Folks had to pledge hard cash if'n they wanted the kids to git a ed'cashun. Me, I run off after three years! Teacher wanted to whup me, an' I was most as big as him. I fetched him a clout up alongside his head with a stool. He fell down like a poleaxed steer. I figgered mebbe I'd kilt him dead, so I stole his horse and lit on outta there. The horse wasn't much. Caved out from under me in less'n twenty miles, so I stole another and kept on a-goin'. Ain't never been back and ain't never stopped stealin' horses.

"Y'know, some folks has gallopin' consumpshun, and others has headaches all the time. Me, I got me a bad case of the horse-thief-itus disease. Ever' time I see me a good-lookin' horse, I jest nach'erly has to own him. Robbin' stages jest ain't my line of work. Reckon that's why I got ketched."

The squire was taking all this in. "Your given name, I

imagine, is taken from that famous James Bowie, who partic-
ipated in the well-known struggle at the Alamo. Am I right?"

"Well, sir," Knott replied, "not 'zactly. You see, Maude,
that place I told you about? Maude is in Bowie County, just
next to Red River County, Bowie bein' named after Jim Bowie.
When I was jest a li'l shaver, folks called me Will, account I
was named after Buckskin Bill Williams, my pa's captain in
the Texas Fourth Brigade. Buckskin and my pa worked together
when they had the mail contract for Red River County, and pa
was Buckskin's right-hand bower. You know, sort of a straw-
boss. Anyways, my pa figgered the sun rose and set in Buckskin
Bill Williams, and when I come along in '41, he saddled me
with the name, William Bill Knott.

"Now li'l boys is ornery critters. I know 'cause I was a
purty bad 'un my own self. Them boys deviled me account of
thet damn name! They'd mock me; 'Bill will not—will Bill,
or will Bill not?' Don't mean all thet much now, but along
then I'd git me a mad on, and I'd chase them boys. Oncet, I
smacked a bigger boy with a leg bone off'n a cow. Liked to
busted his head in. More times than not I'd git whupped!

"I reckon you kin un'erstand how thet'd bother a feller.
Anyways, I jest started callin' myself Bowie Knott, and the
name stuck. I been Bowie Knott ever since."

Brooke looked blank for a moment; then he beamed. "Oh!
Yes! I see what you mean! Dashed awkward, that. Can't say
I blame you for changing it! Will Knott...Hmmm..."

I was thinking to myself. It wouldn't pay to get overly
friendly with these men. After all, they had stuck up my boss's
stage. Anyway, we'd been here for about a half hour, and it
was time to be moving on. I said as much, and we got them
up and headed back toward the stage.

Bowie Knott and his partner, the Cherry Creek Kid, seemed
to be arriving at a decision. They'd started up a whispered
palaver as Brooke and I taken the horses off picket, and as we
neared the coach, they stopped and turned around. Cherry Creek
had something to say.

"We been talkin' it over, McCowan. Last thing we want to
see is thet lady gittin' ketched by Injuns. Or them gittin' any
of us, either. When you said you'd run us down 'n skin the
hide off'n us, I believed you. Sooo...What I'm tryin' to say
is you kin trust us with guns if them Injuns ambush us somewheres along the line. We won't run off! Turns out I'm left
handed, so I kin still shoot. I'd druther you kept quiet about

thet, leastways around thet big Frenchman. He's one mean feller! Like as not, he'd try'n stomp my good hand next if he knew I could still handle a six-gun."

Bowie Knott looked at me slyly. "Ain't sayin' what happens after the fight, if there is one. You purely can't expect us to stick around once we got them guns back. We'll promise you one thing, though. We won't turn 'em on you!"

CHAPTER 5

GRAYSON'S LOOKED MIGHTY GOOD TO ME, SPE-cially when I discovered it was still in one piece! Me'n the chestnut topped out on a rise that looked down on the station, and we were a good twenty minutes ahead of the stage.

The main building was a long, low one, built pretty nearly the same as the smaller Pawnee Station. Squared logs on an unmortared stone foundation. The roof was sod, spread on over pole rafters, and I counted five stovepipes. One must be for the cook stove, I told myself, and the others were for warming up the sleeping rooms.

A high-peaked barn sheltered a spare coach, which I could see to one side of the open double doors. The midpart was a drive-through, with similar double doors open at the other end of the building. Pretty slick arrangement! Teams could be changed, passengers and their baggage could be handled, a coach could be repaired—and all this under shelter, in any weather. Man who laid this out sure used his head for something other than a place to hang his sombrero. You run into all kinds of folks west of the Mississippi. All of 'em the sort that's willing to take a chance. Willing to leave them big towns where everything is all laid out for you just in the hope they'll better themselves. Build a future for both themselves and their families.

I've known grubby miners who had college degrees, barmen with a knowledge of Greek or Latin, and I worked alongside a cowboy whose paw was a British lord. Looking at this well-planned stage station, I'd bet hard money that the man whose talent was plain to see had a background in engineering.

The clang of a hammer on steel identified a smithy on the other side of the barn, and I could see a short, brawny man, wearing a leather apron, working at his anvil. Close by was a youngster pumping the bellows at the forge. The coals had reached an almost white heat when the boy paused and wiped at his forehead. He turned towards the smith, and as he did so, he apparently spotted me. For a moment, he stared, then grabbed the man by the arm and pointed.

As I watched, the smith laid down his hammer, peering upslope, a hand cupped over his eyes. Then the boy taken off, running towards the main building, and the man now held a rifle. He moved back under the overhang of his shop with the heavy forge as a shield. He was ready.

As I once read; "Discretion is the better part of valor," and I figgered to wait for the stage before going down that slope. Could be they'd already had Injun troubles, and the feller might just shoot first and ask his questions later.

The oily squeak and jingle of harness coming up behind me announced the arrival of the stage. Looking back, I saw the leaders really straining to haul the heavy coach up what was little more than a slight grade. I could hear the grunt and slobbering wheeze of horses pushed to their limit, but not a bit more. Ada had done a fine job! She'd nursed those poor critters along and brought in the stage, but not at the expense of six dying horses.

"Don't stop," I called out. "Keep 'em rollin' on down to that barn!"

She nodded, a big grin on her pretty face. "Don't I rate a howdy do or a salute of some kind?" she asked. "Bet you twenty dollars I could take these horses another thirty miles, given three hours to rest 'em!"

I reined the chestnut alongside the coach and followed a few feet to one side. Folks were running out of the station building, and the blacksmith had laid aside his rifle. Ada rolled the coach right up to the barn doors where she stopped and set the brake, handing the lines down to a grizzled old duffer who came out of the barn. He barked an order to a tall, skinny galoot, and together they started unhitching and moving the teams into the barn.

Doc was the first one out of the coach. He caught me as I was climbing down off my horse.

"We got us a problem," he told me. "The man you shot has a great deal of difficulty in breathing, and he's spitting a lot of blood. I'm afraid the lung is filling with blood and other fluids and he'll die unless we can get that ball out of him, and soon. I don't think he'll last to Fort Kearny."

We humans are strange. When I'd shot that man off of the

horse, I'd fully intended to kill him. Now...Now that the
bandit was wounded and might die, I wanted to do all that I
could to help him get well. And Doc, who'd been one of that
gang's victims, was saying the bullet had to come out or he
would surely die!

"I hear you," I told him. "But who's gonna do it? You?
You've already said that you don't have the experience."

"Yes, like I said, I'm not really a doctor. I've not had one
hour of formal medical education. But...I've assisted in similar operations, and I'm willing to give it a try. We have no
other choice. He'll die before we reach the fort."

A middle-aged man with graying hair was standing by the
coach door and overheard our conversation. He held out his
hand. "I'm Grayson," he told us. "I run this station. I couldn't
help hearing what you men were saying. My wife was a nurse
with the Union Army and worked all through the war. I'm
certain sure she'd want to help if you men need her. I can go
and ask her, but in the meantime, get that man out of the coach
and up to the station. We can clear off a table and put a clean
sheet on it. I imagine you'll want a lot of hot water, right?"
Doc nodded, and Grayson trotted off.

I wasn't quite ready to trust Bowie Knott and the Cherry
Creek Kid, so I asked the old hostler where I might lock 'em
up. He pointed towards a small stone building that set by the
two outhouses.

"Smokehouse," he told me. "Door's two inches thick. The
hasp's got a railroad spike stuck through it, so's you don't hafta
worry about them two bustin' out. Ain't the cleanest, but it's
the strongest shed on the place."

I thanked him and taken Knott and the Kid down off their
horses. Ben and the squire were helping Doc lift out *Smith*, or
Jones, whichever one he was. The skinny hostler got them a
two-inch plank, and they used it to carry the wounded man.
Doc walked alongside, carrying his black bag and cautioning
them to be careful.

"You ain't gonna lock us up in there, are yuh?" Knott was
indignant as I swung open the door to the shed. "Why, we'd
never make it through the night! Ain't no damn winders, and
we cain't breathe without we git some air. C'mon, McCowan!
Be a sport! Halloran's got him a hurt hand, and he's a sick
man! Look at all the damn grease on thet floor! Ain't even got
us a place to sit down, much less git any sleep. Have a heart!
We promise we'll not give you no trouble if yuh let us go on

over to the station. 'Sides, we ain't had no eats, and you cain't expect us to *eat* in here. It stinks!"

The Kid kept his mouth shut, but the look he gave me told how he felt. Knott was right! It was pretty bad. I'd no reason to feel sorry for either of them, but . . .

"Aw right!" I gave in reluctantly. "But you two are not exactly payin' passengers, so remember that. C'mon, git goin'! First time you git outta line, I'm not only gonna lock you up in this smokehouse, I'm gonna hogtie you and let yuh roll in the grease like a coupla pigs."

"No!" Knott had held up his manacled hands. "Them cuffs stay on, Mister Knott! You ain't gonna have no trouble with your eatin', and I'll rest easier knowin' they're there. I could cuff you behind your back, so count your blessin's."

I closed the shed door and slid the spike down through a steel loop on the hasp. Halloran had his vest buttoned, and his bad hand was cradled inside. "Thanks, McCowan," he told me. "You're a white man, and I 'preciate you not lockin' us up in thet pig sty of a shed."

"Yeah!" I replied. "I'm a soft-headed fool, that's all I am. Now git along there. Let's see how they're makin' out with your friend. Which one is he? Mister Smith or Mister Jones?" To myself, I was thinking about the Kid's intended, or implied, compliment. That I was a "white man"! Me being half Choctaw and half Virginia English didn't exactly make me white. I knew what he meant, and I reckoned I'd felt the same way if I'd been threatened with being locked up there in that greasy smokehouse.

As we entered the main building, I could see a small knot of people gathered around a sheet-draped table. Ben Chilton was holding a lamp high above the prone figure of the man I had wounded. Doc's front was draped with a sheet, pinned at the neck, and a lady next to him was rigged the same way.

The salesman, Winters, was bent across the feller's feet, holding him down tight, while Rousseau and the stage messenger each held an arm. While I watched, Doc reached out and pinched the feller's chest.

"Can you feel that," he asked. He had pinched real hard!

A muffled groan was all the answer he got. I could smell a strong odor of whiskey, and I reckoned that was all we had for a painkiller.

Doc was sweating now. The lady reached out and wiped a

cloth across his forehead. He was wearing his glasses with a
cord looped across the back of his head.

"I'm ready now," Doc told the others. "As ready as I'll ever
be. Hand me the probe."

There was a basin there, handy to his reach. Steam, from
the boiling water it held, was fogging Doc's glasses, and he
taken a swipe at them with his sleeve. He was trembling.

The lady, whom I figgered must be Grayson's missus, taken
a pair of tongs and fished a long, skinny instrument out of the
basin of boiling water. She handed it over to Doc with a question in her eyes.

"Are you certain that you can manage this?" she asked. "A
wound in that area is—"

"No!" he snapped back. "I'm not certain at all! But I have
to do something, or this man will die. Now! Hold him! If he
moves while I have this probe in the wound, it can be fatal!"

I'm darned if I could stay there and watch him poking in
that feller's chest. I motioned to Knott and the Kid so's they'd
sit down on a bench along the wall, and I sat next to old man
Forney, who was hunched over in a chair. The way he was
favoring his shoulder, I figgered it must hurt real bad.

"How you feelin', Mr. Forney," I asked. "Reckon that's a
dumb question, but it's all I can think of right now. That
shoulder must be givin' you fits, I reckon. Could you stand a
drink of whiskey? They must have some, less'n they poured
it all into that feller on the table. Let me scout around a bit
and see what I can come up with."

The feller I'd shot in the leg was sitting close by with a cup
of coffee in his hand. He crooked his finger at me, a grin on
his freckled face. "Whiskey's over there, under the counter,"
he told me. "Wouldn't mind jest a smidgin in this here coffee,
if you don't mind. This laig's hurtin' me real bad! Reckon the
doc will dig this slug outta me? It feel's like it's rubbin' ag'in
the bone. Got me half sick. Likker might jest take away thet
uneasy feelin'."

"I'll ask the doc when he's done with your friend." The
man was lucky he hadn't bled out, I thought to myself. And
also lucky the ball hadn't broke the bone. Doc had a wadded
compress on the wound, and it was stained red, but holding.

Grayson was behind the counter, and he poured me a drink
from a bottle that was about half full. "You got any more?" I
asked him.

"Sure," he replied. "I make it myself. Got a coupla big barrels full out in back. Why? You got you a big thirst?"

I explained about Forney, and he handed me another glass. "Take that bottle on over," he said. "I'll fetch out more."

The old man looked mighty grateful when I handed him the glass Grayson had poured for me. He tipped her back, and it went down in one long swallow.

"Thanks," he said huskily. "Can't say as I've ever tasted any better. How about you? Are you a teetotalin' man?"

"Not lately," I replied. Putting an action to the words, I poured myself a good, long drink and drank it on down. I can't say it was the best I'd ever drank, but it sure did do the job! Knott and the Kid were looking longingly at us, so I went on over, stopping on the way to pour in the 'smidgin' that feller had wanted in his coffee. Again, that freckled, weatherbeaten face crinkled up in a smile.

"Thanks, McCowan. This is jest the medicine I need!"

"What we all need," I told him, "is some grub, and soon. Then we're headin' out towards Fort Kearny." I paused. "You sure you want Doc pokin' around in that hole in your leg? I figger we'll be at Kearny by this time tomorrow. There an army doctor can treat it and do a proper job."

He shifted his weight in the chair and grimaced. "Hurts like hell, McCowan! Got me half sick to my stomach. Bouncin' around in thet coach feels like somebody's jabbin' with a red-hot runnin' iron. I'll take my chance with ol' Doc!"

I poured him another smidgin from the bottle. "Well, the whole thing's up to Doc. I'll ask him when he gits through with your friend."

Turning to leave, I got me an idea. "By the way"—this in a somber tone—"jest in case Doc ain't able to save your pal, what name do we put on the headboard?"

He looked his surprise. "Why, Gunnison! Frank Gunnison is his name. I figgered you knowed thet." He was suddenly apprehensive. "You mean he might not make it? Gosh! Never figgered he was thet bad off!"

Sitting taller in the chair, he craned his neck over that way. "Knew he was hit hard, but not makin' it... Hey! He'n I been ridin' together four years now. Garth and Gunnison! Hell! We was jest two cowpokes with the same notions other fellers like us had from time to time. Needed cash to start. Even worked out a brand we would use someday. Double G! A pair of 'em, back to back. Makes a good-lookin' brand. Had a notion to

put a stake together and buy us a small outfit. Place far enough
from here where we wasn't known. Raise us some beef and
mebbe trap wild hosses. Never hurt nobody we was robbin'.
Now Frank's mebbe dyin'..."

I knew what he meant. Reckon we all of us feel the temptation at least once in our lives. See some feller that's no
smarter'n us who's living high on the hog. We know that all
it takes is some money and a few good breaks and there we'd
be, owning our own place. Only it just don't work out that
way! Somebody, somewhere along the line, has to lose.

There I was! Feeling sorry again, and for the guys who'd
tried to hold us up! Like I said, we humans are strange and
contrary critters.

"What do your friends call you, Garth?" I asked him as I
poured him another shot of the whiskey.

He grinned and tousled his red hair. "What else? Me, I been
Red Garth as long as I can remember." The grin faded, and
he leaned forward. "See how Doc's comin' with Frank. I would
be obliged to yuh! And ask him about my laig."

I told him I'd do what I could. Went over to where Knott
and the Kid were sitting and gave them each a swig from the
bottle. "Gonna see what I can do about rustlin' up grub," I
told them. "You fellers sit tight and keep out of the way."

Back at the table, Doc and his helper had their heads together, bent over the wounded man. I stood next to Chilton
and asked him how they were making out.

"Shhh," he whispered. "He's about to take out the bullet
now." His arm, holding up the lamp, was trembling with fa-
tigue, and the cords in his neck were standing out with strain.

"Want me to take over for a spell," I asked. "You gotta be
'bout wore out, holdin' that light like that. Here, let me take
it. You go sit down for a while."

"I'm fine," he whispered back. "Just fine. Now shut that
trap of yours and keep it shut!"

Just then, Doc straightened up, a triumphant smile on his
face. "We got it," he said quietly. "Now all that remains is to
clean out the wound and apply the bandage." He turned towards
Grayson's missus. "May I please have the whiskey now?" he
asked. "And I'll need a cotton swab. But first..." He tipped
up the bottle and taken a long swallow.

"Aahhh!" his face was red, and sweat made a wet ring all
around his collar. "I wanted that before I started to cut, but I
didn't dare! Can you imagine? I did it! I really did it! All it

took was determination and the knowledge that a man would die if I didn't at least try."

Deftly, he probed into the wound with the cotton held in a pair of tweezers, then rinsed the area around the opening.

"There, now, Mrs. Grayson. If you would be so kind as to apply the bandages, I believe I will sit down. Suddenly, my legs feel very weak..." He started to sag.

Rousseau grabbed him on one side, and the messenger taken the other arm. Someone brought a chair, and he relaxed into it. He still held the bottle and started to take a swallow from it.

"Whoa on there, Doc," I called out. "You got you another patient if you feel up to doin' some more cuttin'. Best to hold off 'til you got him fixed up. Then you can drink her dry if you care to. Right now, a clear head is needful."

I explained about Red Garth and the pain he was feeling. "Says it feels like that ball's scrapin' the bone. Reckon mebbe you could take a look, Doc? Now that you've had some practice, this one oughta be a gut cinch."

He agreed to take a look at least, and I went over where Grayson was standing, behind the bar. I explained about our reasons for driving on through to Fort Kearny and asked him if we could get something to eat before we left.

"You mean you're not staying over," he asked. "Surely a night's sleep would be the best medicine for everybody. Now that Doc has taken care of your emergency, there's no reason for speed. Stay the night, and start fresh in the morning."

Suddenly, something I'd had in the back of my mind needed an answer. The way that youngster had acted when he had seen me on the hill and the blacksmith's having a rifle so close at hand. I was sure that Ada must have told him about the attacks on the stations at Otoe and Pawnee and wondered why he hadn't questioned me for more detailed information.

"Have you folks had any problems with Injuns in the last day or so? How about the southbound stages? Any trouble on their runs? Have they seen any Injuns wearin' paint?"

"Nope!" he replied. "No trouble here. We've always been ready for them, and I guess they know that. Counting myself, we have five men here and three women. Plenty of guns and enough ammunition to hold off an army. These log buildings and the way they're squared off makes this almost as tight as any fort and would be very easy to defend. We've had our share of Indians who come here and beg for food, and we've never turned them down. Once or twice, we've had some bucks who were feeling their oats and got a bit quarrelsome. The blacksmith cooled 'em down. He's a dead shot with a rifle, and he's strong as any bull. They'd settle down in a hurry once he'd flexed his muscles.

"As for the southbound stages, there hasn't been one for more than two weeks. Wells, Fargo had the section shut down because it was losing money, and they'd offered it for sale. This run of yours is the first we've seen since they closed it down and transferred the drivers to stations out West.

"As to what has happened at Pawnee," he went on, "that's just terrible! They must have been caught completely unprepared! Such a nice, young couple, too. And the hostler, he was the girl's brother. They've only had the station twelve weeks. Came out from Ohio, I believe, and planned to settle down on a farm. This job was a temporary one. Just until a nest egg was built up so they could buy supplies and tools."

Remembering the slain pair in the grove, I told him how I had come upon them. "One seemed some younger than the feller I found pinned to the tree. He'd been cut up, and they taken his scalp. The older man wasn't savaged none, and his knife was still in his hand. Had a lot of blood on it, so I reckon he fought 'em right up to the last.

"You got any idea who them fellers might be, Mr. Grayson? Also, might there be some way you could git down there so's them fellers could git a proper burial?" I explained having no shovel and no way to get them underground. It had to be some twenty-two miles from here, since I'd found them about three miles north of the station at Otoe.

He nodded. "I know who they must be, all right. What I can't figure out is how they were taken. Sam Ledger had to be the older man. Sam's been around for fifty years! Maybe even longer than that. He was one of the old mountain men.

"Some say he was all through the northern lands, trapping beaver and trading with the Indians, even long before Lewis and Clark made their explorations. He claimed he had been a drummer boy during our Revolutionary days and came west to the mountains right after peace with the British. He called them the shining mountains! Told me that in the morning, before the sun got high, he could see those mountains shine two hundred miles before he'd reached the foothills.

"Sam was as crafty as any Indian, and it's hard to understand

how he could be ambushed. Course, he was getting old, and
his hearing wasn't all that good anymore.

"The younger man was a pure greenhorn! An artist! Had a
notion to paint Indians, and Sam had promised to take him to
an Arapaho encampment, just about thirty miles south of this
station. His partner warned him against going out, 'specially
since he had to leave his sick Indian wife."

"His partner? Where's that partner now?" I asked. "Does
he live somewhere's around here, close by?"

"I thought you knew." He answered my question with lifted
brows. "Why, he's in that cabin, next to the barn. Sam's Arapaho wife is there with him. She's mighty sick! We done all
we could for her, but she ain't responding. Sam's partner is
an oldtimer they call Isatay. It's a Kiowa name he picked up
years ago. The old man's flatulent and offensive as hell. I guess
he has no control over it, but he can sure make you wish that
you were nowhere near him. *Isatay* means Rear End of a Wolf.
Indians named him, and it sure stuck!"

I had to smile. Injuns had a way of really nailing sign when
they put a name to a body. Last year, we'd had us two young
Kiowa boys try to steal horses from our corral out in back.
One was called *Ape-má-dlte*, Struck His Head Against a Tree.
Gosh knows when, or where, he'd done it, but it surely left
an impression, because it became his proper name.

"Well," I said. "I 'preciate you tellin' me all about the old
man, but you still haven't answered my question. S'pose you're
gonna be able to bury them fellers, Christian-like?"

"Not only that," he replied, "but we'll bring them here, and
see they have a regular funeral. We already have eleven buried
in our little plot. Most of them from a party of emigrants that
the Sioux attacked west of here. Don't worry! I'll see that
they're taken care of, McCowan." Grayson had his hand stuck
out as he said that. We shook on it, and I felt some reassured.

"Looks like everythin's under control here," I told him. "I'd
'preciate it very much if'n you'd git some grub on the table
so's these folks can eat. I'll be back here soon. I reckon I'll
go talk to Ledger's partner. Tell him what happened to Sam
and the greenhorn."

He nodded, and I taken off towards the door. Over in the
corner, I saw Ada, and she was playing with the little girl.
Somewhere she'd rounded up a rag doll, and the poor little
tyke was laughing and hugging that doll something fierce.

CHAPTER 6

ault him the same, but I seen he was wearin' no rifle gun

THE CABIN WAS IN BACK OF THE BLACKSMITH SHOP, and I found it with no trouble. Smoke was coming out of a pipe that was right-angled out of the back wall. I taken time to knock on the plank door, and it was just as well that I did.

From inside, I heard two clicks as a hammer was drawn to full cock and a harsh voice asking, "Who'n hell is that, and why in hell d'ye have need of me?"

"Name's McCowan!" I hollered back. "Want to talk to you, and it's about your partner Sam. I ain't got no gun; least not in my hand, I ain't. C'mon! I want to talk peaceable. You hold off now! I'm comin' in there, so hold your fire!"

Grayson was right! The inside of that cabin smelled like a boar's den! The old man put up his long rifle soon's I'd showed him my hands was empty. I could see the figure of an Indian woman, lying on a cot against the wall. She stirred as I came in and raised up on an elbow to peer at me, then fell back soon's she saw I was a stranger. Her cheekbones, high-planed and angular, thrust sharply against the tautness of her drawn features, seeming ready to pierce the fragility of the dusky, copper-penny skin. Her clothing hung loosely, and an exposed arm was thin and almost fleshless. Her neck was swollen and darker-hued, her breathing difficult.

The old feller looked more like a bear than a man. What he was wearing was deerskins, with the hair left on. Stocky built, he was of medium height and seemed mighty spry. His white-flecked beard was full and almost to his eyes. Right now, them eyes was looking me over, and none too friendly.

"Like I said outside, my name's McCowan. 'Fraid I got a mite of bad news for you, old-timer. About three miles this side of Otoe Station, I found your pard and a young feller. They'd been badly used by Injuns, cep'n them Injuns sure had some respect for Sam and showed it. He still had his hair!

50

T'other feller had been cut up some, but readin' the sign, I figgered old Sam had stood up to 'em right to the last. He had him a knife in his left hand, and his face was some powder burnt. Looked like he'd dared 'em to git in close so's to count coup on him, then cut right and left, slashin' them Injuns guts out 'til one of 'em pinned him with a lance.

"Matter of fact," I went on, "he had blood splashed over him, and his left arm was red, clean to the elbow! Too much blood to be his own. Some of them Injuns was mortal cut!

"They left him his knife, but I seen no sign of his rifle gun. I s'pect they taken it along. Right now, some brave's braggin' to his womenfolks how he snatched it away from old Sam. Mayhap them same womenfolks is wrappin' up some cuts and slash wounds. That is, if he taken that gun whilst Sam was still breathin', which I doubt."

The old man hung his head. Then he glanced up, and his eyes were bright with moisture. "Old sonofabitch! Done tolt him not to go out there! Them Sioux! They've had it in fer him ever since he stole this here woman." He pointed, his chin whiskers jutting in the direction of the cot.

"Must be nigh eight year now. Wo-ista, there, is Arapaho. One of the *Nakasinena* folk. The 'Sagebrush People.' I b'lieve they mostly come from around the Colorado Springs.

"Her name means Charity," he continued. "Lass is shorely thet! Always tryin' to he'p folks. Give you the last bite or the last sip, then hand you her only blanket. She'n some of her band were camped on the *Cache le Poudre*; you know, on Powder River. They got jumped by a party of Ogalallah* Sioux braves. Charity was a young'un then. 'Bout sixteen year's old. And she was a purty thing, with ever'thin' in just the right places, and a plenty of it.

"Well, sir . . ." He'd fished a stubby pipe outta a pocket in the breast of his hunting shirt and lit it with a splinter he'd taken from the fireplace. Once he had it going, he repeated . . . "Well, sir, there was a buck in thet bunch thet was called Crow Dog. He's a chief now, but then he was jest an up-and-comin' warrior. He taken a shine to Wo-ista here, a real shine! Wanted her bad! Real moon struck, he was.

"Red Cloud put a high price on her, but finally Crow Dog,

---

* "Ogalallah" is an 1868 spelling; "Oglala" a modern one.

with his family he'pin', come up with the bride price. He'd stole hisself a fine spotted-assed pony from the Nez Percé Injuns, and thet was part of what he had to pay. Imagine it was like pullin' one of his eyeteeth to part with thet fine spotted hoss, but he did! Tied the hoss in front of old Red Cloud's tipi and went on home to wait fer his bride."

Looked like the old man wanted to talk, so I rolled me up a smoke and settled back on my hunkers to listen. Just as I got it fired up, old Isatay broke wind, grunted what might have been an apology, and continued his story.

"Now Sam had been back there in Red Cloud's camp when my l'il friend here was brought in. He'd been dickerin' fer an old Hawken rifle with a busted lock, and him and Red Cloud was close to a trade. Sam seen this here gal and fell jest ass-over-teapot in love with her. Couldn't live 'thout her to woman up with him. So he studied on how to steal her."

"It was comin' on nightfall when Crow Dog brought up the pony. Red Cloud taken his time 'bout noticin' it was there. Walked out of his tipi, right past thet pony, and perambulated over to visit with some friends.

"Sam seen his chance . . . Grabbed thet gal and got her up behind him on thet Nez Percé hoss. Then he taken on out like the demons a' hell was right on his heels! Got hisself plump away from thet camp afore they'd even knowed what had happened. Near rode thet pony into the ground, but made our camp afore thet hoss give out. We quick like packed all our plunder and headed south fer our health. Bein's our hosses was fresh, them Sioux never come close. They tracked us fer the rest of thet week, then give up and went on back. Crow Dog never forgot and shore never forgive old Sam."

In the brief glimpse I'd gotten of the woman, I could see that she might have been beautiful before she taken sick. A thought occurred to me that possibly Doc Talbot might be of some help. After all, she was still a young woman. Sixteen, eight years back, meant she was only twenty-four now. That swelling in her neck could be something with which he'd have some experience. I mentioned that to old Isatay.

"One of the stage passengers is a fair hand at doctorin' and might jest figger out what's wrong with the lady. Ain't no real doctor, but say's he was a surgeon's assistant durin' the war. 'Bout half hour back, he taken a ball outta an outlaw I plugged whilst he and his pards was tryin' to take over the stage. Worth a try, wouldn't you say?"

He nodded, but his expression told me he held little hope for the woman's recovery. "I'm forgettin' my manners cause I'm mighty beholden to you, McCowan. Where d'ye say they ketched old Sam and thet artist feller?"

"Bunch of willows," I told him. "Jest a few big cottonwoods. Little creek meanderin' through there. I'd say that grove was no more'n three miles this side of Otoe Station."

Remembering the knife I'd found upcreek, I fished it from my chap's pocket. "You ever seen you a knife like this?" I handed it over to him. His face cracked in a smile, or more like a grimace. He weighed it in his hand and peered close at the carved buffalo head on the knife's pommel.

"Sioux!" he told me. "Ogalallah Sioux! From the Buffalo Clan. Them's Red Cloud's 'Bad Faces,' as the rest of Brulé and Ogalallah calls 'em. Old Red Cloud's got hisself mebbe 250 lodges, with close on to 450 women, kids, and old folks. Set 'em up in the game country, east of Fort Laramie, but my guess is most of thet game has been e't by now, and they be startin' on dogs'n horses. Yes, sir! Them as was left there in the village is starvin', whilst Red Cloud and them young bucks of his'n are killin' folks and burnin' 'em out.

"Jest the other day," he went on, "I run into a scoutin' party from the Fifth Volunteers; that's Colonel Maynadier's outfit, outta Fort Laramie. Told me Red Cloud's got more'n three hundred feisty young bucks with him, and ain't been but three weeks back, they plumb wiped out a wagon train of emigrants headed fer the Oregon country. Caught 'em no more'n twenty mile west of Fort Kearny and wiped 'em out! Run off the hosses and burnt the wagons. Butchered their cow critters and e't 'em right on the spot. Had themselves a time, they did, and prac'ly under the noses of the U.S. Army!"

He taken another look at the knife, running his finger along the lines of the carving. "D'ye pick up this stabber in thet grove where Sam and the youngster was kilt?"

"No, sir, I didn't," I replied. "Picked it up alongside a creek mebbe eight miles back from here." I went on to explain how the band that had wiped out Pawnee Station met up with the larger party and turned towards the north.

"Least two hundred, mebbe more, in that bunch. Seen some shod horse sign along with the barefoot ponys. Figgered it must be saddle stock they'd run off from some ranches along their track. Found oats in some of the droppin's, so they'd time enough to use the rancher's feed. Means they must have killed them folks, else they'd been in more of a hurry."

Isatay nodded his grizzled old head. "Son, Red Cloud, with three hundred screechin', bloodthirsty bucks can take his time. Hell! Who's gonna stand up to him? Far's thet goes, they'd take over Fort Kearny 'thout much trouble if he taken a notion. Mebbe couldn't hold it fer long, but he could do it!

"Right now, there's mebbe two thousand Ogalallahs scattered 'round these parts. Most of 'em are peaceable right now, but they is all hongry and needful of clothes and blankets. They is scared the army's gonna send a bunch of soldiers out here to ketch up Red Cloud and treat all Injuns the same. So they hunker up in their tipis, starvin', 'cause they are 'fraid to send out huntin' parties to git game. Big Mouth's camped on Horse Creek with p'raps three hundred in his band. Spotted Tail, old Swift Bear, Iron Shell, Man-That-Walks-in-the-Ground—all of them Ogalallah chiefs are holed up with their womenfolk and young'uns, waitin' fer the army to ketch Red Cloud so's the rest of 'em can start breathin' easy again. Agent Patrick, at Fort Laramie, and Colonel Taylor, in Omaha City, have both told 'em they'll git beef cattle, beans, and blankets soon! So they go on waitin' and starvin'. They ain't gonna wait much longer! If'n thet feller back in Washington don't make up his mind purty quick, blood's gonna run in the territory like nobody's ever seen before. You mark my words, son!"

His voice had been rising steadily as he spoke, and this last ended in almost a screech. Embarrassed, he turned away from me and began packing his pipe. I waited until he had tamped it to his satisfaction, then offered him a light. He puffed away, still avoiding my eyes.

"Well . . ." I said. "Reckon I'd best go see what's happenin' with the stage folks. You want me to ask Doc Talbot if he'll come take a look-see at the lady? Can't do no harm."

He nodded, still afraid to trust his voice, I reckon. So I got back on my feet and walked towards the door. With my hand on the knob, I turned and faced him. "Isatay," I said, "I'm purely sorry about what happened to your pard Sam. He went like a man, you can b'lieve that! He wasn't needful of apologies when he showed up at them pearly gates. I'm hopin' I can do as well when my time runs out." I closed that door mighty softly as I went out.

Ada was seated at one end of a long table as I came back into the stage station. She waved and pointed to the empty chair beside her. Her plate held a moderate-size portion of what looked like stew, and she was drinking steaming coffee cautiously from a thick white mug.

"Come sit here by me, cowboy," she said. "We've got some things to talk over, and now's as good a time as any."

"I could use some grub," I told her. "And that coffee is first on the list. Be right back!" I figgered to have just a sip of that whiskey before I sat down to eat. Grayson was still behind the bar, so I headed that way.

"Did you find old Isatay, all right," he asked as he set a bottle and glass on the bar. His face was reddened, and I figgered he'd been hitting the jug himself. All this exciting news and having an operation take place in his station, plus the first stage he'd serviced since Wells Fargo closed down this branch . . . I didn't blame him for taking a sip or drinking a whole darn bottle, for that matter.

"Yep," I replied. "Saw the Injun lady, too. She's purty sick. Look's to be starvin', she's so skinny. Thought we'd give Doc a chance to see her. Whatever's wrong, I reckon it ain't respondin' to old remedies. She don't look like she's gonna live much longer if somethin' isn't done, and soon."

I poured myself a good stiff shot and drank it on down. Surprisingly, it wasn't all that bad. Smooth, for homemade likker. Grayson had said earlier that he made it himself and had a couple of barrelsful out in back. By this time, I felt really hungry, and I asked him about supper.

"Did them others leave anything? Whatever you got handy, give me a double helping, and I could sure stand some coffee along with it. Matter of fact, if it takes any fixin', I'll be willin' to wait if you could spare that coffee now."

"Elk stew," he told me. "That's all we got, but that elk was shot just yesterday, so it's nice'n fresh. My old woman puts together a mighty fine stew, 'specially when she has garden-fresh vegetables, like now. I'll bring it on over to you, so go ahead and sit yourself down. Pour another drink, and take it with you."

Sounded good to me! I poured another, but this time taken a bit less than before. Carrying the glass, I headed towards the table and Ada, with whom I did want to palaver. Hadn't had a chance up 'til now, and after all, she was my boss.

Didn't really look until I got real close, and I was not too pleased to find Ben Chilton sitting in my chair. He and Ada had their heads close together, and both were chattering away like a pair of lonesome magpies on a back-yard fence.

"S'cuse me, cap'n," I said, nudgin' him with an elbow. "I do b'lieve you've done set yourself down in the wrong chair. Happens I'd planned to sit in that exact same chair myself, so why don't you just run along and find yourself some good listener who likes to hear 'bout all your adventures on the seven seas. 'Specially 'bout all them little brown gals out there in them islands. The ones you was tellin' me about."

Had to give him credit. He never so much as batted his eye. Just set back in the chair and looked up at me.

"You mean when you were telling me about how cooperative and easy to get along with you had found the Kiowa girls in Texas? I have to admit you were one up on me. After all, I had only *seen* the girls in the islands, while you . . . Right! I perhaps do have the wrong chair! I'm getting up now."

He'd seen the glint in my eye, I reckon, and saw the shot of whiskey tipping over his head. Hastily, he shoved back a bit and stood up, his eyes on a level with mine.

"I do believe you would have, McCowan, and that would only lead to more of the same. By all means, sit down. Don't imagine you've had your supper as yet, and I don't want you to go hungry. If you'll excuse me . . ." With an inclination of his head, he turned and walked towards the bar.

Ada was grinning when I did sit down. Didn't say a darn thing for a minute. Just sat there looking me over with an eyebrow cocked quizzically and the grin still showing.

"Well," I asked, "what's so dern funny? After all, you'd ask me to come sit down. Said you had somethin' you wanted to talk about. Well . . . Talk!"

"McCowan," she said, "you're not only rude, you're also a bit childish. Why jump all over Ben when he sat down here at my suggestion? It has always been my belief that two or more heads are better than one. I've been trying to make my decision about that little girl, and I merely asked for some advice from him. Mrs. Grayson tells me that she has no living relatives now that her parents are dead. The other man was her uncle, and he was unmarried."

"Oh!" I said. Then . . . "Well, maybe I did jump the gun a mite. I'm sorry, Ada, and I'll mebbe apologize to Ben later on. What is it you're tryin' to decide?"

"The Grayson's are childless, and she would like to have a child, even if it were adopted. They've asked me to let her

remain here with them, and they'll give her a good home. Do
you think I should, McCowan?"

"Look, Ada, my name's Rush, and I'd answer to that quick
as I will McCowan. I know that right now you're my boss,
but I'd sorta like to keep it friendly if'n you don't mind. I
reckon I hadn't thought much about the little girl. We've had
other things to worry about. Grayson seem's to be doin' all
right here, and his wife is nice enough.

"Besides," I went on, "who else is there to take her? I know
you're not in the market for a daughter, not havin' any husband
and all . . ." An awful thought had just crossed over my mind.
"You ain't got one, have you? Surely, you ain't a married lady,
are you, Ada?"

Her frown would have withered ripened wheat. "And what
makes you think that I'm not married, *Mister* McCowan? Is it
because I'm not attractive and not ladylike for the likes of you?
Because I can drive a stage as well as any man, or even better
then most men?" She'd stood up now, and I seen a pulse
pumping away in the hollow of her throat. A throat thickened
and red now, with the flush rising.

"Why, hellsfire . . . I mean, gosh no, Ada! Just calm down,
now! Dammit, Ada! You know what I'm tryin' to say. Just
that I'd figgered you were single and lookin' around . . . No! I
didn't mean that, either! What I mean is . . . Aw, hell! No matter
what I say, I gotta wind up with my boot in my mouth! Please,
Ada! Just sit down for a minute and start all over again. Please!"

She was starting to giggle now. The flush remained on her
pretty face, but for a different reason. I reached out, taken her
by the arm, and sat her back in her chair.

"What it boils down to, Ada . . . Heck! I was taken to you
the first time I laid eyes on you. I mean that! Course, we had
our little differences right from the start, but we got all that
straightened out, didn't we? So let's at least be friends, and
mebbe later, when all this is behind us, we can talk some more.
Okay?"

She nodded, and the smile on her face was something else!
"Sure, Rush! When we get back to Atchison, we'll talk about
it. One more thing . . . Take it easy on Ben, will you? He's
really not a bad fellow, and he admires you."

Well, I doubted that, but I wouldn't say no more about it
now. I told Ada about the Injun lady, and right away she agreed
that we should ask Talbot to take a look at her.

"Another thing, Ada. If we're gonna drive on through, we

should git things ready. You go ahead and talk to Doc. The
cabin's easy to find, but hunt me up so's I can go along."

As I walked towards the bar where I planned to ask about
harnessing the fresh teams, I started thinking about what my
friend Isatay had said. How Red Cloud was running with three
hundred bucks and nobody being able to stand up to him. Hell!
The station here was not as safe as I figgered it'd be. Injuns
wouldn't pay no mind to even twenty guns, not if they had as
many men as that. Best we'd be on our way, and the sooner
I saw the gates at Fort Kearny, the better I'd feel.

Rousseau and Squire Brooke had their heads together, with
drinks on the bar in front of them. As I came up, they both
turned and offered to buy. Got insistent, even!

"Thanks," I said, "but right now I'm more interested in
gettin' that stage ready to roll out. Right now we're well fed
and rested, and things look like they might just go fine for us.
I just talked with an old Injun fighter who said a band of three
hundred bloodthirsty Sioux are out there, with a pretty bad old
chief leadin' 'em. Red Cloud!

"Now, I don't know 'bout you two, but I just as soon find
myself in the middle of Texas right now. Anywhere, just so
long's I don't have to pilot a bunch of greenhorns through a
passel of scalp-hungry Injuns. Howsomever, I hired on, so I
reckon I'm stuck with the job. I could use a bit of help in
gettin' ready."

Naturally, the Englisher was the first to move. Rousseau
was a loner, and that was plain to see. A big man, he'd had
no reason to lean on anybody. Killed his own snakes, and he
didn't take readily to orders. I could understand, being an old
he-wolf myself. Grudgingly, Rousseau downed his drink and
followed us out of the station.

The blacksmith and the skinny hostler showed us where the
harness had been hung, and together we got them three teams
harnessed up and hooked onto the stage. The chestnut seemed
to be pretty well rested, so I decided to take a chance.

"Marvelous," Brooke told me. "You'd ran her literally, a
hair's-breadth from death, but here she is, all ready to run. It's
all in the bloodline, I would imagine. With good blood in her
breeding, she'd naturally be a winner!"

Ada and the doc showed up about then, and trailing behind
was Ben Chilton. It was just as well. I needed someone who
could bully the rest into getting ready to pull out, and Ben was
perfect for that.

"We're gonna take Doc to see the Injun lady," I told him. "Then, soon's possible, we're headin' out for the fort. Take Brooke and Rousseau with you and explain it to them. We'll get back to you soon's Doc's done examining this lady, so I would appreciate you havin' them ready to load up the stage. Can you handle that?" He nodded, and we left the room.

This time, I didn't hear no rifle being cocked, and Isatay let us into the cabin quick enough. Apparently, he'd spoke to Wo-ista already 'cause she was sitting up against a long roll of blankets placed at the head of the bed.

Doc called for more light, and he had her lie down flat. Carefully, he ran his forefinger under her jaw line and back behind her ears. "Bring that lamp in real close," he asked. "Now, miss. If you'll open your mouth wide as can be. Ah! That's it . . . All right. Thank you, miss." He turned back, his forehead wrinkled in a frown. "Remove the light. Relax now, miss. You may lie back down."

Doc turned around and stared at me'n Ada McAlister. His expression was bleak, and he seemed to be trying to find the right words. "This began," he told us, "as a simple case of tonsilitis. Lacking treatment, the organs have become so swollen that she has been unable to swallow food. This has brought her to the point of starvation. Unless I help, this woman will die. I couldn't stand something like that lying on my conscience. I would not be able to forgive myself.

"Before I can remove the tonsils, I must first reduce the swelling, and that will take time. I know that you are both anxious to leave this place and continue on to Fort Kearny, so I've decided to stay here. Wait!" He held up his hands as both Ada and I started to protest.

"It doesn't really make any difference to me. I have not really decided where I want to practice. When I started out on this trip, I'd planned to travel until I found some place that appealed to me. Some little town that had a need for a man with my experience. So here I am, and I have a patient who needs me in order to survive. I'd be a fool if I left here now! So go ahead and leave me here. I'll be fine!"

What could we say? There was no question as to his being right. Wo-ista *would* die unless she could eat. Doc wasn't a big man in stature, but he sure had my respect!

"Besides, that wounded bandit can't be moved safely. A bad jar could open up his wound, and we both know stages are notorious for bumpy rides. No! I'll stay, and you must let me assume responsibility for Gunnison. Frank Gunnison, that is his name, isn't it? I'll make sure a lawman takes him in custody as soon as he's fit to ride."

I reached out and taken his hand. Gravely, he accepted, and a big smiled flashed across his face. "It's been a privilege, Mr. McCowan," he told me. "A real privilege to watch you in action. You're a fighter, you are, a real fighter!"

"And you are, too, Doctor Talbot," I replied. "You ain't needin' no excuses, believe me. You take care now, y'hear!"

We made our good-byes to Isatay and Wo-ista. Ada had been sitting on the cot, talking with her, and now she reached on over to hug her. I was struck by her contrasts. Not more than two hours ago, she was tooling that heavy Concord along a rutted road, confident in her ability to handle those six big horses; now she was purely feminine and comforting this poor, gravely ill woman with unmistakable sincerity.

Wo-ista looked up at me with eyes that seemed too big for her thin, bony face. "Thank you," she said. "Thank you all for caring that I live. But you . . . You, who looks like my brother. I thank you for telling me of my husband's bravery in battle." A tear appeared at the corner of each eye, only to be wiped away immediately.

Sitting straighter, she squared her pitifully thin shoulders and reached out for my hand. "May you walk in safety on every trail, my brother. Here!" She laid a small deerskin bag in my palm. It was beaded, with the head of a bird worked out in tiny blue and white beads, and had a thong on one end. The bird's beak was sharply hooked, like that of a hawk or an eagle.

"Wear this medicine and no man can strike you down," she told me. "It was my father's, and his father's before him. It is very old and very powerful and belongs with a brave and powerful man."

I nodded and slipped it around my neck. "I thank you, my little sister. When we come back this way, I want you to be rid of this sickness and beautiful again. Don't be scared, because this white man is your friend, and he will help you as he has helped others today."

CHAPTER 7

HUNCHED OVER IN MY SADDLE, I SHIVERED DEEPER into the old brush jacket I'd dug outta my bedroll. Late September mornings were chilly in Nebraska, 'specially in the hour just before sunrise. For a Texas cowboy, it seemed durn cold!

Behind us, at Kiowa Station, we'd exchanged teams for the third time since leaving Grayson's. Ahead of us some four miles was the swing station on the Little Blue. There we'd change again and head for Liberty Farm, where we'd find hot coffee and breakfast; with luck, no more'n three hours away.

I had to marvel at Ada's pluck. Traveling at night over a strange road, she'd still managed to average five miles an hour. Earlier on, I'd noticed that she'd made no efforts to avoid chuckholes and such in the roadway, and I'd asked her why. Seemed like she wanted the passengers to be joggled.

"Simple," she told me. "If I constantly steer around the bumps during the day, the horses will expect to be steered. At night, I can't see the road, so I obviously wouldn't know where those obstacles are and won't try to avoid them. The teams would be confused." She looked down at me with her mischievous grin, bent forward on the seat, her arms sawing back and forth to the motions of the lines.

"Last thing I'd want to do," she said, "is to confuse my beautiful horses." Her face was flushed, and her eyes sparkled with the joy of living. My lady boss was getting prettier every minute, and I was a gone goose! Leastways, she'd got over being mad at me, and we were friends. That was at least a good beginning!

As me'n the squire loped along behind the stage, I began reviewing the last two days and thinking about the future. My prospects weren't all that bad. I had money in the bank both in Texas and in Kansas City. Wasn't no way I could be considered handsome, but I was young and healthy. My knowledge

61

of ranching, and now the marketing of beef cattle, had to stand me in good stead. I could certainly support a wife and family. That was another thing. I wondered whether a smart, independent girl like Ada would want children. Her having all that schooling, mebbe she wouldn't want kids taking up her time. Aw! That was nonsense! Every girl wanted to have a husband and some children of her own.

Sure! Ada had lots more education, and she'd traveled around the country more'n me. She had manners and knew how to handle herself in polite company. But then again, if we did marry, we'd be living on the ranch in the Val Verde, and polite company was few and far between. Good manners might not be all that important cep'n just as common courtesy.

Ben Chilton seemed to have enjoyed an education, and this was not common with those who followed the sea. Course, being's he was a captain, I reckoned he was bound to have seen some schooling. He was riding in the coach right now, having himself a little nap, I supposed.

Frank Forney had stayed behind at Grayson's. Made up his mind at the last minute and told me why. "I doubt I'll see any better doctorin' at the fort," he'd said. "Talbot's got a head on his shoulders and knows what he's doin'. 'Sides, I ain't all that bad hurt, nohow, and you folks can pick me up on your way back to Atchison. Jest save me a seat!"

So only ten of us had gone along with the stage. Ada, of course, was driving, while Sam Goodson rode shotgun. Squire Brooke had elected to ride horseback alongside me. Inside, we sat the three bandits on the front seat, facing rearward, while Chilton, Rousseau, and Lou Winters kept an eye on them from the back seat. Bowie Knott had complained about riding backwards. Said it made him dizzy and sick to his stomach. Red Garth and the Cherry Creek Kid didn't seem to mind, and the Kid warned Knott about what would happen should he give in to the nausea. Garth added a few choice words of his own.

Winters was armed with two of the pistols we'd taken off of the bandits. Ben held the Triplett & Scott rifle and an army-model Colt he'd appropriated right after the holdup, a fine .44 six-shooter. The gambler, Rousseau, still carried a revolver in his armpit rig and the bandit's shotgun, a cut-barreled 10-gauge. As we were pulling out, Grayson had said we looked more like an armed posse than peaceable citizens.

Well, when we reached the fort, I could turn them bandits over to the military, and our passengers could make the connection with the westbound stage. We'd have us a day, mebbe, before having to start back to Atchison. I doubted that there would be much to see at Kearny, but at least we'd have some time together. Me 'n Ada, that is.

A holler from the squire brought me out of my reverie. I glanced over and saw he was pointing ahead. A rider was on the road ahead of us, and he was sure enough making a cloud of dust build up behind him. Ada was already slowing down a bit when I pulled alongside and motioned to her to pull up the teams. Heads were peering out of the coach windows, and Chilton asked why we were stopping.

"Just sit right where you are 'til we find out what this feller has to say," I warned him. "He's all by his lonesome, so we have nothin' to fear from him. By gollies! He's sure enough runnin' that horse flat out! Can't have come far, at least not on that animal. Must of got him fresh at the station on the Little Blue. 'Nother mile or two and he'll not have a horse left to ride. That one'll be wind-broke or on the ground dead! You boys keep them ears open and listen so's I don't have to repeat what he says."

The horse, a big buckskin, didn't want to stop now. His blood was up, and he come off the ground, his forefeet pawing at the sky as the rider hauled back on the reins. A full minute went by as he struggled to get control; then he jumped to the ground.

"Injuns!" He gasped for breath. "Burnin'! Killin'! They be headed this way. You gotta turn back! Hun'reds of 'em!"

He sank down, sprawling on the ground, the reins still in his fist and the horse pulling away. Brooke must have read my mind. Quick like, he gigged his horse alongside of that buckskin and grabbed the cheek plate of the bridle, holding until the horse calmed down.

It was then I noticed blood on the man's pants leg. It was low down, and there was a jagged tear by his calf. When I stepped down off the chestnut and taken a look, he pushed my hand away.

"Ain't nothin' but a scratch," he said. "Don't pay it no mind. Give me a minute to catch my breath . . . Say! You men got any drinkin' water? I could sure use some! Been ridin' most all night . . . Plumb forgot back there at the station."

Ada handed down a canteen, and I got the cap off and let him drink. He taken a few big gulps, then poured some over the back of his neck. He shook his head and smiled.

"Hmmm... That's some better, believe me. Reckon I can't git nothin' stronger, so this'll have to do. Ahhh! Feelin' better already..." He tipped back the canteen and taken a couple more swallows.

"What's all this about Injuns?" I asked. "Where and how many did you see? How far've you come?"

He stood up and handed me back the canteen. His eyes, a pair of reddened spots in his dust-caked face, were drilling straight into mine as he answered.

"More'n I ever want to see again," he told me. "Cheyenne and Sioux—hun'erds of 'em! I run into 'em near the Summit Station, more'n fifty miles back. Barely got outta there in time! They come from the direction of Hook's, so I reckon a body can figger that's gone, too.

"They been right behind me most of the way. Agent over at Summit give me a fresh horse and told me to warn all the stations along the line. I've done my best..." Here, a bit out of breath, he had to stop. He drew in a big lungful and went on.

"At every station, I've warned the folks, grabbed a fresh horse, and been on my way. Each time, couple miles out, the smoke starts risin' up again. I was barely ahead of 'em at Thirty-two Mile Creek. Taken a saddled horse and left mine behind. Done a bit better gittin' to Lone Tree. Had me some coffee, and a chunk of bread I ate on the run."

"How about Liberty Farm?" He seemed dazed, so I taken aholt of his arm and shook him. "What about Liberty Farm? Did they burn Liberty Farm? C'mon, man! Answer me! Surely there's enough men there to hold off the redskins!"

It seemed like he hadn't even heard me. "Gotta git goin'," he mumbled. "You folks better turn back. Ain't the chance of a snowball in hell of you gittin' through. Gotta git goin' my own self. Gotta warn folks."

I reached out and smacked him a good one with the flat of my hand. He reeled back, stumbled, and fell to the dirt. A look of shock quickly changed to anger, and he clawed at his holstered gun. "What'ja wanna do thet for," he cried. "I'm bustin' my butt tryin' to help you folks, and you gotta go'n hit me! Had enough! I'll sho you what's what."

Quickly, I knelt and grabbed his gun hand. "Sorry, but I had to do that. You were talkin', but you weren't makin' no sense. Now! I'm gonna let you up, and let's start all over again. What about Liberty Farm? Are they all right?"

He nodded. "Give me a hand up," he asked. Then he said, "They might've held out for a time. There was 'leven or twelve at Liberty Farm, seven of 'em growed men. Couple of the kids was big enough to shoot a gun . . . Them women can probably shoot, too.

"It's thirteen miles from there down to the Little Blue, just ahead of you there. I wasn't no more'n halfway when I looked back and I seen smoke. Now it might've been some of the shacks I seen burnin'. Mebbe they're still holdin' out in the station, but I doubt it, mister. Has to be least three, four hun'red Injuns in that bunch. Young bucks with paint on their faces and blood in their eyes. How long you think them folks is gonna hold out ag'in that many Injuns?"

What he said made sense, but we weren't gonna panic. The Indians *would* get us if we lost our heads and just started running. Thing was to have a plan. That also made sense!

"Look," I told him, "you git back on that horse and go, but slow down! We don't see no smoke over the station ahead of us, so they must still be at Liberty Farm. Your horse is gonna quit on you if you run him hard like that. Stay at a fast walk less'n you do see Injuns behind you. We're gonna figger out our own plan right now. Ride careful, y'hear!"

I helped him on the buckskin, and he was off again, but at a lope, not the hard gallop of before. Chilton and the rest had all piled out of the coach and was wanting to know what I'd figger to do now. I singled out Ada and spoke to her. "We gotta have fresh horses before we start goin' anywhere. If you'll take the coach into the grove of willows over there and stay hid for a while, me'n the squire will see if we can do somethin' about that. Okay? Make sure nobody smokes or makes any noise. I'm countin' on you to keep 'em calm."

I'd spotted the willows earlier, about a half mile off of the stage road. Willows meant water, and they were at least tall and thick enough to hide the coach from anybody on the stage road. My plan wasn't all worked out yet, but I figgered we'd play it through as we went along.

"How's about lettin' us have our guns?" It was Bowie doing the talking, and he didn't seem scared or nothing. The other two nodded as he asked me the question. "We done told you the truth. We ain't gonna use 'em ag'in you or these others."

I turned to Ben Chilton. "If Brooke and I aren't back, say, in an hour, go ahead and let them have guns. I'm makin' you boss over this bunch, together with Miss McAlister. The stage

might have to be left behind. There's only six horses pullin'
this stage, and there's eight of you. So you might plan about
how you'd double up if the coach's left behind."

"What are you planning, Rush?" It was Ada, and she had
a look of uncertainty on her face. The first one I'd seen. I
wasn't so sure whether I liked that or not, but uncertainty hadn't
seemed to be her long suit, and I knew I could depend on her
grit. There were a couple I wasn't sure of, but that lady boss
of mine wasn't one of them!

"Squire and I . . ." I turned towards him and grinned. "I
guess I volunteered you without even askin'. You might not
be all that willin' when I tell you what I got in mind.

"Even if we decide to turn back to Atchison, we'll need a
change of teams. Not right now, but soon. So . . . While you
folks are hidin' out in the willows, me'n the squire will be
scoutin' out the station on the Little Blue. If things work out,
we'll be back, and real soon, with three new teams. I don't
have to tell you to be on the lookout for Injuns. And you,
Garth! I'm makin' you a sergeant, so to speak. You're in charge
of yourself and your two friends under Cap'n Ben and Miss
McAlister. If somethin' *does* go wrong, I'll figger it was your
fault, and it's *you* I'll be comin' after. Everybody understand
that? Fine! We're on our way!"

We held the horses down to a fast, running walk. Once, I
turned around just in time to see the stage going under the trees
and out of sight. The sun was out now, and I'd begun to feel
warm again. Taking off the brush jacket, I remarked to Brooke
on what a fine day it was turning out to be.

He gave me another of those funny smiles of his and said
he agreed. "With the exception, sir, of the close proximity of
those blasted heathen. We had an identical problem back in
India. The beggars never knew when they'd been beaten!"

CHAPTER 8

WE TOPPED OUT ON A LOW BLUFF ABOUT TWENTY minutes later, one overlooking the line of trees that marked the river. On the far bank, I could just make out a squat building set in under the trees. A thin tendril of smoke rose from one end, but I saw no activity. Nobody was moving around.

To one side, a corral held a number of horses, and it all appeared to be normal and peaceful. "Take it slow'n easy, Tom," I told the squire. First time I'd called him by what I knew to be his proper name, and it surprised me. I reckon asking him to share what could be dangerous made him seem a closer friend. I'd read Thomas Brooke, Esq., on the manifest passenger list, but until now "Squire" or "Brooke" had seemed proper. Funny thing, I'd never figgered them British. I mean, what I'd always heard about 'em back home. They were s'posed to be standoffish. You know. Sort of filled up with their own importance. Leastways, that'd always been the way we figgered. Now here come this feller Brooke, about as typical a Britisher as you could ever find, and he turns out to have more guts than a government mule. Quiet, sure enough, but long on nerve. I volunteer him for a scout in Injun country, and he just grins and trots right along.

I snuck a look at him from under my hat brim, and I could tell he was some excited. Not a bit scared, just expectant and happy to be doing something new and different. Mebbe I could get him to talk more about India. I had me an idea he could tell some real stories if he taken the notion.

The bluff was almost straight down, but being mostly just loose dirt, the horses squatted and slid to the bottom. We rode across the flats with our rifles at the ready. Horses could sense the tension, and the chestnut had his ears flipped forwards, stepping dainty in the loose, sandy soil.

Full daylight now, and we made easy targets out on them

bottoms. Nobody challenged us, which seemed mighty strange. The hostlers not only should be on the lookout, but it seemed likely they would be jittery and ready to shoot anything that moved. Most fellers *would* be right after being warned of a pending attack by Injuns. Most would shoot first, then ask the questions. At least that had been my experience.

Brooke and I were riding about twenty feet apart so's to not make it any easier by bunching up. Not a sound could be heard other than the normal ones of nature. Not a sign the hostlers had even spotted us. Overhead, a pair of pigeons passed us, low down, at about treetop level, their wings in spasmodic flutter. Across the river, several willows housed several hundred blackbirds, their noisy chirping extra loud in the early-morning air. It was a hidebound cinch that no Injuns were creeping through them willows or hiding in some brush clump, ready to pounce on us and lift our hair.

At the river, we paused and scanned the opposite shore a full three minutes. Nothing! The stage road forded across by following a shallow bar, fetlock deep on the horses. Tom stayed back at my suggestion while I walked the chestnut a ways out onto the bar. Still nothing!

I turned around and signed for him to follow me, but not too fast. Easy . . . easy . . . I signed. Take it slow and easy! Once across, I got into the trees and turned to watch, the Henry cocked and ready.

Suddenly, Brooke's horse shied and jumped sideways. I saw a spout of water kick up close to him and then heard the dull boom of a large-bore rifle.

"Git outta there," I hollered. "Git under cover! There's somebody tryin' to kill you!"

Brooke drove his spurless heels into the horse's ribs as another bullet kicked up the water just beyond him and the second report crashed out. Down in the tangle of trees, I'd no chance of seeing where the shots were coming from, but it sure wasn't no big bunch of Injuns. Not with just one rifle doing the shooting. Injuns would be splattering that water 'til it looked like a hailstorm. No, this was just one man with a single-shot rifle that taken time to reload. That's why the shots were spaced. A third shot struck right at the water's edge as Brooke gained the shelter of the trees.

Once under cover, he trotted his horse over to where mine was standing. "Whew! That *was* rather close, wasn't it! We *should* investigate, shouldn't we?" Here he paused and very carefully let down the hammer of his cocked Springfield. "I am afraid I didn't see anyone to shoot at," he told me ruefully. "It wasn't the Indians, though, was it? They'd shoot more times than that bugger did; given the chance, that is. My, I felt dreadfully alone out there! Nowhere to hide in the middle of a river." He grinned. "Did feel good in a way. Got the blood to pumping rather fast, don't you know?"

He taken a deep breath about then and held it, then let it all out in a gasp. "Huh! Does keen up one's senses, old boy; good for the digestion. I haven't felt quite so alert since my days in India." He looked at me and laughed. "My word, aren't I the talkative one! Does that, don't you know? When one escapes from danger, seems he feels compelled to do a *lot* of talking. Don't ask me why! Experienced it before, especially one Sunday morning. At Meerut, the large station south of the Punjab. I'll tell you, if you don't mind.

"We had a mixed bag of troops there. Mine, Her Majesty's Sixtieth Rifles, of course, plus the carabineers and two troops of horse artillery. The native troops were Bengals—cavalry and infantry. Three troops, in all, of those buggers I told you about. The ones with a distaste for pork in any form.

"We were turning out for church parade when it all began there; the mutiny, that is. Dressed in our best white uniforms, of course. The beggars opened fire on us from behind excellent cover. Not that it mattered, since we were unarmed. Fortunately, my Rifles had not reached the church. Had we been inside, they could have slaughtered us like so many cattle. It would have been a literal trap.

"Sergeant major kept his head. Splendid chap! Absolutely fearless, he was. Helped me get my men in order and under arms again. With a few well-placed volleys, we routed the beggars, but not without terrible loss to our own.

"I must confess, I felt totally naked out there. Had the sergeant major not been there to steady us all, it might not have gone well for us. It is so easy to panic in a situation like that. I . . ." He paused, and his face was darkened with the beginnings of a flush. "I say! You must think me a complete ass for gibbering away like this! Please don't think too badly of me, McCowan. It's unforgivable, I know, but I haven't stood fire for several years."

I didn't dare laugh, but I had to bite my tongue. Brooke was really embarrassed. Most men would have still been running after an experience like he'd just gone through. Here he

was apologizing. Well, I figgered, the less said, the better.
Besides, we were running out of time.

"We'll lead our horses," I told him. "First off, a check of
the station building. Let's make it fast, 'cause we're on that
one-hour limit I mentioned to Ben Chilton. He'll figger somethin's up and give them bandits their guns. C'mon! Let's take
a look inside that cabin."

It only taken a few minutes to reach the edge of the wagon
yard. From there, it was plain bare ground right up to the front
door. If that rifleman was still around, we might just get shot
at crossing that open clearing.

"Wait here in the trees," I told Tom. "Keep your eyes on
that hillside behind the cabin. If our friend tries another shot,
you'll spot him by the powder smoke. Lay some shots in close
and mebbe you can keep his head down. Ready? I'm on my
way!" I taken off, running bent over towards the door of the
station.

I made it across the clearing without a shot being fired.
Once at the door, I didn't hesitate; just pushed down on the
latch and went on through. The one big room was empty!

There were signs of a hasty departure. Clothing and the like
were scattered on the floor near two bunks. Cupboard doors
hung open, and dried beans littered a counter and the floor
below. An empty whiskey bottle lay there, also.

I went to the door and called to Tom. "Leave the horses
there," I hollered. "Tie 'em up short so's they can't jerk free.
Then c'mon over here, and don't stop to pick flowers along
the way. Make it quick!"

Moments later, he came through the door and taken a look
at the mess left behind. "My word," he said. "They *were* in
somewhat of a hurry, weren't they?" He paused. "Isn't it possible they might have been the ones who shot at us? The hostlers, I mean. Obviously, they were frightened when the other
fellow brought word of the Indians. This mess they've left
behind would indicate they were perturbed. Perhaps we looked
like Indians to them. Frightened men will do strange things.
To them, everyone looks like the enemy."

I nodded grimly. "Yeah," I agreed. "More'n likely they
were the ones, all right. They were so scared they'd never even
though about runnin' off the horses. Left 'em for the Injuns as
a present. Fine for us, though, 'cause we sure do need 'em.
Let's take a quick look for something we can use; in the way
of food, that is. Grab that feed sack there and see what we can

find to put in it. Like that part slab of a side of bacon on the counter. And here's some beans and a couple cans of peaches."

We rummaged around and managed to find several more airtights with fruits and vegetables inside. Under one bed, I found a full bottle of brandy and showed it to Tom. "I say! That's a bit of luck!" He beamed as he put it in the sack.

"Okay! Let's go put leads on some of them horses. Might have trouble hazin' 'em loose, 'specially with the possibility of somebody mebbe takin' potshots at us. You go on with the sack and bring our horses to the barn. I'll be lookin' for halters and some rope. Take care, now. Keep an eye on that hill behind us. We're close enough that them damn fools should be able to tell us from redskins, but you never know. 'Specially with me bein' part Injun," I muttered.

I found a dozen halters in the barn and several coils of manila rope, and by the time Tom got there, I had rigged out several of the horses. I picked the best of the lot.

"We'll take eight," I told him. "And we'll drive the rest ahead as we lead ours out. No sense in leavin' none here. That'll give us six fresh stage horses and a couple extra in case we have to leave the stage behind. Everybody'll git a horse to ride, so there'll be no need to double up."

Taken only ten more minutes to catch up the rest and put halters on them. These horses were pretty tame. Wasn't like catching up a saddle horse of a morning. I'd be having not just one but all of them horses trying to get away; then, in most cases, the one you wanted was hiding behind them others, like he could read your mind. Many's the time I've been so dern mad I could shoot that horse. 'Specially after I'd be knocked down and stepped on by the others.

Once the haltering was completed, we were ready to leave. I had two leads rigged out, with four horses on each, when I remembered something pretty important. Feed! Grain for not only these fresh animals but also the ones now hitched onto the stage. I explained to Tom Brooke.

"I seen some pack saddles in the barn. We'll use the two extra horses and load 'em pretty good for no more'n we got to travel, back to where we left the stage. Oughta be able, properly rigged, to load four hundred pounds on each of them horses."

The saddles I'd seen were what we called "sawbucks," made sorta like that handy tool for cutting stove wood. The close cousin to an Injun's saddle, it was basically just two forks of wood connected with wooden side bars. Taken no more'n a few minutes to rig one on a horse. The tough part came with convincing the horse that pack on his back wasn't a grizzly or something just as bad. If push came to shove, best thing to do was to tie up one foot and blindfold the horse.

"Learned this in the army," I told Tom, looking back over my shoulder as I settled the saddle on the horse's back. "A little old feller no bigger'n a minute taught me all that I needed to know. He sure had a lot of stories to tell and reckon he told me every one. Said he learned how to throw a diamond hitch from old Jim Bridger. Reckon you've heard of him?" Tom nodded, and I went on.

"There was times when our outfit had to prac'ly live off the land. You know; foragin' for our eats and carryin' all the feed for our animals." I paused and looked around.

"Hand me them two bands over there. Yeah, them two. We call that one in your right hand a 'breeching' band, and the other is a 'breast' band, which sorta explains itself. They keep the saddle from shiftin' forward or back on the horse. Thanks, Tom. Let's see, where was I, now? Oh, yeah . . . The old feller could tie the derndest things on a horse's back. Odd-shaped things that you'd figger couldn't conform to the shape of that horse and stay on. That's the important part of all this. Makin' 'em stay on!

"You gotta figger that the horse might have to go through heavy brush where branches could scrape off your load; then there's uphill and downhill, and believe me, once that pack starts to slip, it's all over." I turned and grinned. "I mean that literal like. It's usually strewed from one end to the other!"

Luckily for us, the mixed oats and barley was in fifty-pound sacks. There were some canvas tarps draped over a partition between stalls, and I taken one and showed Tom how we could use it. "Be lots better if we had panniers. Them's just a sorta flat-sided bag made outta canvas. We'd just hook 'em to the forks and carry the grain sacks inside. We can make do with these tarps, though, and I'll show you how."

Working quickly, we hung the tarps from the forks, making deep folds on both sides of the animal's back. Both tarps, made from heavy sailcloth, had metal-reinforced eyelets next to the edges, and that helped a whole lot.

As Brooke loaded the bags into the drooping folds, I drew up on the rope I'd rigged through the eyelets. It was sorta like tying store-bought shoes, I reckoned.

"Now comes the part you gotta watch," I told Tom. "Takes two men to really do it right, though you can do it by yourself if you know how. This is what that old man called his 'Bridger' hitch! First off, you take one of these straps he called a lashing cinch. Notice that it has a solid ring on the one end and a hook on the other."

"Now it'll take about fifty, sixty feet of rope to lash down the pack, so we'll cut off, say, sixty feet or so. To measure off that length, we'll use what we call *brasada* down Texas way. I'm six-three, so my arm spread is about the same, and each time my arms stretch out this rope, I'm measurin' a mite more'n that six feet in length. Doin' this ten times gives us close to sixty feet of rope. That make sense to you?"

Tom nodded and watched with interest as I measured that amount of rope. "I've seen that done before," he said. "But never really knew that principle of height versus reach."

"Now," I went on, "we tie one end to the ring, and passing the cinch under the horse's belly, we reach across for a turn around the hook. Next, we bring the rope back and let it pass through the ring. Now we have a double line passed across, and we pull it up snugly.

"Okay! Next, we flip a loop of the running line back on around the pack. I reckon that's why they say you 'throw' a hitch. With your free hand, take the doubled rope and give it a couple twists; pull the running end through the middle and throw another loop around the pack. Back on through the middle again; throw another loop and bring the running end back through the ring. Now all we gotta do is tighten this whole thingamabob and we got her done!"

"Most fellers are satisfied to just draw her tight, first off, then tie off on the ring. Me! I learned better listening to that old man. Watch! I come around to the off side of the horse, reach up over, and take aholt of the loop that passes over the front of the pack near the horse's neck. I twist it twice and put a bight of this running line in that loop. Now when I haul down, I've doubled the leverage on my line, and it'll never come loose accident'ly. Then! I make the final tie, and we're all done!"

We packed the second horse, with Tom making all the loops and twists. It taken him a little longer to get the hang of it, but he finished in fine style. He was very pleased and thanked me for showing him how it was done.

"I figger everything is worth learnin'," I told him. "You

never know when something might just come in handy. Now! We better git back to the stage, or them folks'll think we runned off and left 'em behind."

It taken us a while to find a way up the steep bluff, but we finally did. It led back and forth several times, doubling in hairpin turns to reach the top. Once up there, the first thing I did was to survey the horizon to the north.

"I don't see any smoke, do you, Tom?" I asked. "It's only thirteen miles from here to Liberty Farm. If the buildings were all on fire, we'd sure as heck see the smoke. What the feller must have seen was a small outbuilding or two the Injuns had touched off. Anyways... Look's like we might be safe for a spell at least."

Twenty minutes of steady riding brought us to where I had asked Ada to hide the stage. After everybody had said their glad-to-see and the like, we switched harness to the horses we'd brought along and put the others out on a picket. The whole bunch said they could sure use something to eat, so we got a small fire started and put coffee on to boil. Wasn't really much there for a meal, but with bacon frying and the prospect of hot coffee, soon everybody was pretty cheerful.

Tom was telling about being shot at when I taken Ada off a ways so's we could talk without being interrupted. "The station on the Little Blue had been abandoned when we rode in," I told her. "Could be one of 'em hung around and the shots fired at Brooke came from him. We never did see anybody, and sure looked like they left in one heck of a hurry. It's somethin' you'll have to consider," I said. "When this Injun trouble is over and you git the stages to runnin', we may have trouble findin' folks to man the stations."

She smiled. "Have you noticed that you're using 'we'?" she asked. "Don't mistake what I am saying. If you've made up your mind to stay with us for a while, I'm very happy. I need a strong man by my side, Rush. One who isn't afraid to *do* something without a big discussion beforehand. It seems to be a prevailing trait amongst men who are city-bred. We think alike, you and I, and we both agree a strong position is an excellent one to bargain from."

"To be honest, Ada, I really don't know what I want to do. Right now, I mean. I have an interest in my family's ranch back in Texas, and I probably should be there right now. I know more about cattle than anything else, and I like working around 'em. Good money, too, if you know what you're in for and don't mind doin' it.

"My folks and I made a bundle on the drive last year and could have done it again. I had my reasons for not wantin' to go back right away, but now . . . I dunno, Ada . . . I'd invest some cash in your stage line, but I don't think you want that, do you? Not that I blame you. Lots of folks are real good friends until they try working together or get involved in a partnership. Most always comes out the same way; a misunderstandin' turns into a big fuss, and then they aren't even friends anymore. I wouldn't want that to happen, Ada. Not to you'n me. Not now, when we've got such a good start. I care, Ada . . . I really care!"

She was standing pretty close, and it just seemed natural to put my arms around her and draw her up close. She leaned against me for a moment, then started to pull away.

"I don't want it to happen like this, Rush. Not out here on the prairie where most anyone could walk by and see us. Please! Wait until we are back in civilization and can see each other with some degree of privacy."

"Hey!" I said. "Right now just think of me as your big, protectin' brother. Nothin' wrong with a brother and sister huggin' each other." I grinned down at her. Then, slowly, I bent my head and kissed her softly. Tenderly, I cradled her in my arms, and her soft warmth responded urgently!

She raised her lips, and one hand went behind my head to press our lips together tightly. I could hear a roaring in my ears as we slowly sank down into the fragrant blue stem that carpeted the prairie. The tightness in my chest became almost unbearable, and I struggled to breathe. I tore at my collar as my neck swelled from the heightened pressure and felt relief as the button gave way.

One of us groaned. The sky reddened behind my eyelids, and the earth rocked beneath our bodies as our lips met and clung. We were lovers, alone in a world of blue skies and fragrant flowers. A world that dipped and spun.

Then, slowly, our world came back into focus, and I gently loosed her arms from around my neck. "You're right!" My words came with some difficulty. "There is a time, and this isn't the right one for either of us. When this is over, my sweet Ada, when this is all behind us, then I'll find words that tell how I feel about you. Until then, we'll play this out according to the Book."

On my knees, I brushed the hair back from her sweet face and kissed her eyes, her cheeks, and those tender lips.

"Oh, my dearest," she murmured. "I do care for you, Rush! Right or wrong, I wanted you then. More than I dare tell! But we can wait. It's worth waiting for, Rush!"

CHAPTER 9

"**T**HERE IS ANOTHER WAY," I TOLD THEM. WE were gathered around the cook fire, sipping coffee and trying to make some decision about our next destination.

"I looked at a map," I went on. "Back at Atchison, there was one on the wall of the stage station, and it showed this route and also the land around it. Now the Little Blue is runnin' a little to the north of our stage road. It crosses, or runs, under a bridge on the road from Fort Kearny east to Nebraska City. If we could follow the river, we'd come onto the old Holladay Overland road, about thirty miles east from the fort.

"It'd mean we'd be addin' some miles to our journey; however, it'd be easy goin' from that bridge to the fort. What do you folks think? How about you, Ada?"

"Sounds good to me, Rush. We can't follow our own road no matter what. Going south, we might run into more Indians, and we'll have some trouble finding fresh horses. I say we try the river! After all, I'm the one who's responsible for you passengers, since my uncle and I own the stage line. So what do we do first, Rush? Your idea, so you're the boss!"

I'd glanced around the fire as Ada made her little talk, and I figgered everyone who counted was with us. The three bandits didn't really have a say-so, but I'd have listened.

"First off," I told them, "we'll grain these horses. We can shift the grain to the back boot and put what's left up on top after we're done feedin' them. Give the new teams a regular portion but double up on the one's that pulled this stage here. We'll trail them and the two extra horses on behind, 'cause we're gonna need 'em.

"Now if we were follerin' our regular schedule, the next change would be at Lone Tree, fifteen miles ahead. So we'll change teams every three hours, mebbe every two. We'll have to wait and see just how rough the goin' will be. It ain't gonna be no regular road, so it could be awful tough on them horses."

"*Mister* Rousseau!" I called out to the gambler, who'd had very little to say on this trip. "I imagine you'd ruther a horse was under you than to ride that stage. Grab onto the saddle we put up there on top. Slap it on one of these here horses that we brought back. The less weight we have loaded in that coach, the easier it's gonna be to pull."

Bowie Knott held up his hand. "How's about me, Mc-Cowan? How's chances for me to git outta here? Ain't no reason for me to ride this here stage. I ain't no invalid!"

"Right as rain, Mister Knott. Climb on outta there. Git your saddle outta the boot and make it quick. Time we rattled our hocks on outta this place! How about you, redhead? Now that bullet's outta your leg, reckon you could stay on a horse for a while." Garth had struck me as a fair man, with some principle to him. The others seemed to look to him as their leader, and I was gonna have to trust them 'til dark, anyways. Might just as well go all the way.

He was already climbing out of the stage. He winced, and I knew that grin wasn't coming easy. "I'm ready to take a stab at it," he replied. "But I figger that long's you trust us to ride, you might's well give us back them guns. Injuns won't wait for us to put on a gun. They never heard nothin' 'bout that gunfighter's code of honor. You got my word, and the boys'll go along with it. We won't try to make a break. Leastways, not until this Injun trouble is way behind us."

My mind was already made up. "You hang right there for a spell, and we'll saddle your horse. I'm gonna have to git this gun business straightened out, and it'll take a minute. Right now, I got yours parceled out to them as didn't own a gun of their own, and I have to figger how to make sure that everyone stays armed. What gun was yours to begin with?"

"The army Colt the cap'n has in his belt, and thet shotgun, too, but thet might's well stay on the stage. Good gun for a feller thet ain't much of a shot. Can't hardly miss a target up close, and it usually does the job."

That sounded easy enough, so I asked Ben to hand over the Colt, plus the powder flask and bullet pouch that went with it, and gave the whole works to Garth. He thrust it down in the holster he was still wearing after making sure the caps were all in place.

"I got me an extra cylinder," he said. "Here in my shirt,

where it's handy to the reach. Saves time when you need it loaded in a hurry." He was right! Many fellers did it, and that included me. Sometimes we'd dip 'em in paraffin, and that would make 'em waterproof and help keep caps in place.

Winters had two navy Colts that had once belonged to our talkative bandit, Bowie Knott. He admittedly wasn't much of a hand with a gun, so I traded him the shotgun. With it, he could be reasonably sure of hitting something. One of them I gave back to Knott, and the other went to Ben Chilton. He had the Triplett & Scott rifle, so I didn't bother about any extra loads for the belt gun. He'd do better with a rifle.

"Here, Bowie," I said. "You're gonna have to git along on just one of these navys, but you can take the powder and the bullet bag. You got you one of them cylinders planted away somewheres?" He nodded and held up two fingers!

The Cherry Creek Kid was sitting in the coach, looking as cheerful as I'd seen him yet. "Jest gimme back my two old Remingtons," he said. "Gonna be nigh to impossible for me to reload 'em because of this busted hand, but if you'll stuff loads into the spare chambers, I'll have me twelve shots."

What he was referring to was that most of us had an empty chamber under the hammer to prevent an accidental discharge. That could happen easy enough if the gun dropped to the ground. It meant you were carrying a five-shooter instead of one that shot six, but it was much safer.

One of his Remingtons was in my belt, and Tom Brooke carried the other in one of the Kid's belt rigs. Hearing that, Tom unbuckled the belt and handed me the outfit. "I have a pocket weapon," he told me, and I watched as he dug it out. A Sharps four-barreled derringer, he'd had it in his vest pocket all along. Lucky for him he hadn't tried to use it.

"It's not a real Sharps," he said, "but rather a Tipping and Lawden copy. They do a rather nice job, don't you agree? I purchased this one at their factory in Birmingham. Their license to produce the weapon comes from Christian Sharps, I was told, and he requires that they adhere to his own close tolerances. This one is in .30 rim-fire, and with the multiple shots, it is a very effective firearm. I should like to keep this short rifle if you don't mind. Must confess that I've never been very good with a pistol, don't you know, and obviously this tiny one would not perform well at far range. However, in close quarters, it would be deadly! Please note that I have cut a cross in the bullet's point. This results in a simply horrible exit wound! We found it necessary to do this in India. As a matter of fact, our arsenal at Dum Dum, just northeast of Calcutta, manufactured the service bullets with similar points. Even a small caliber such as this is capable of stopping a man. I know from experience."

I had thought about handing Bowie's pepperbox to Tom, but reckoned he had no need for it. Since Ada had no weapon, it would do her just fine. I handed it over after explaining briefly how it worked. She thanked me and smiled sweetly.

"I hope I never have to use it, Rush," she said. "But it will be right here if I do need it." She tucked it away in a pocket of her coat, a man's mackinaw she'd borrowed to fit over her traveling dress. One thing ... You'd never mistake her for a man no matter how bulky the coat.

Didn't take long to load the extra chambers for the Kid's Remingtons, and I gave them back to him. I had several more cylinders and offered him one, but he turned it down.

"Doubt I could make the exchange," he told me. "Being one-handed now, it's awkward as hell to do most anythin'. Sure do thank you for the offer, though. Don't worry none, 'cause I'll do my share. Like I told you, I'm left-handed."

Well, it looked like we were about ready. The horses had all been fed, the new teams hitched to the stage, and all of the spare horses tied on behind. Ben Chilton, Rousseau, and Tom Brooke formed the guard around the coach. I taken Garth along with me, and we rode point about two hundred yards in front. Coming on to noon now, and it was uncomfortably hot in the willow thickets. I'd long since removed my coat and tied it behind the saddle's cantle. Garth had little to say about being assigned to the scout detail; he merely nodded and climbed aboard the horse we'd saddled for him. We'd rode in silence for mebbe half an hour when he glanced over towards me. I couldn't see his eyes, but he had a half smile that turned up the corners of his mouth.

"Thet's my horse there," he said laconically. "Thet one you're ridin', I mean. Purty nice horse, wouldn't you say?"

Hell! I'd been hoping the chestnut belonged to Gunnison, the man I'd shot in the chest. At the time, I hadn't really paid much attention to the horse he was on. To tell the upstanding and real-out truth, I'd grown pretty fond of my new mount and figgered mebbe I'd just hang onto him.

"Don't s'pose you'd be open to a trade," I asked. "After all, though I hate bringing it up, you might just be lookin' at

ten years in the pen. Be a shame to have this fine horse wind
up with some court clerk or a fat-bellied deputy that wouldn't
really appreciate him. Leastways, if I was to have him, you'd
be sure he was out where the air is sweet and no city stink's
around. Where the green grass was underfoot to nibble on and
not hard paved streets with busted bottles and the like scattered
around."

He was grinning now and shaking his head. "McCowan, it
seem's to me there's laws ag'in fellers like you. A mighty thin
line t'wixt what you put a bullet into me for doin' to the stage
line and what you're tryin' to do right now. You can't just
divvy up my plunder 'cause I held up a stage. A feller has
some rights, you know."

The grin was fading. He looked down at his hands, that
playful mood changing now to a somber one. "Feller can sure
git hisself into a peck of trouble, can't he." It was not a question,
but rather a statement of fact.

"Reckon you noticed the brand on thet horse. The Runnin'
W! You acquainted with it?" When I shook my head, he continued.

"That there's Cap'n King's mark. Him and a feller called
Kenedy had themselves a fine layout down Nueces County
way. Me'n the boys all worked for 'em, and it was a damn
fine job to hang on to. I mean, you had to toe the line, but
King was a fair man and treated us square.

"We brought a good-sized herd up to Abilene earlier this
year, and I went as *segundo*, under Charley Fry, trail boss on
the drive. Kenedy's the one given me the job, and he said I
might jest look forward to that extra twenty dollars, steady like,
if I kept my nose clean."

He shook his head as if to clear it and went on. "The drive
went through slicker'n grease. Them critters gained a pound
or two, and we tallied a full count at the yards. My first day
in Abilene, I taken one drink. *One*, mind you, and I hustled
back out to the herd so's to make certain nothin' went wrong.
I wanted me thet job, and I was bound to keep a tight rope on
my goin's on."

"Well?" I asked. "What happened? How come you ain't
back there in Texas holdin' down that good job?"

His face was bleak as he reached into his pocket for the
makings and started rolling a smoke.

"Went to the telegraph office with Charley Fry. Figgered
to send off a wire and let 'em know the good news. There's

nothin' like good news to cheer up a feller. They had a bit of news for us. A telegram from Mifflin Kenedy.

"Said him and Cap'n King has busted up their partnership. Said all bets were off as far as any jobs waitin' for us in Nueces. Leastways, no jobs for saddle bums like me who had some crazy idea 'bout gittin' up in the world. We could all keep one horse and take a ten-dollar bonus for doin' a good job on the drive. Said hirin' and firin' was up to King in the future and the *segundo*'s job was filled.

"I blew my whole payoff the first night. Not even sure what it went for 'sides whiskey. Woke up layin' in mud, my head likin' to bust and one two-bit piece in my pocket. On one arm, I had me a gal's garter, so I mebbe had more'n just whiskey, but I sure don't remember nothin'. Frank Gunnison and the Kid staked me to breakfast. Me'n Bowie Knott. Old Bowie was in the same shape cep'n he hadn't no quarter."

I listened, knowing how easy it could have been for me'n others like me to be in the same fix. Disappointments and hard likker go together somehow, and one makes the other an easy trap to fall into. Hadn't been for Charley Canfield, I might be in the same fix right now.

That letter from Julia telling me things were over. That she'd married my brother Milo and would love me like a big brother . . . I could just as easy have got myself drunk, blew my stake, and gone on the owl hoot like these boys.

"The boys and me figgered on ridin' out towards Californy way and try our luck, but we were needin' trail money. I'd even lost my roundup bed 'cause I forgot to take it off the wagon. Sooo . . . We held up the stage, or tried to. Would've been on our way west right now wasn't for you happenin' by to stop us." There wasn't any rancor in his voice. He knew right was right and wrong was nobody, like paw used to say.

"When we git where we're goin'," he told me, "then we'll talk out a deal. Cash money would probably be best, since I would be needful of tobacco and suchlike, but we'd be smart to wait. Some buck's mebbe gonna be toppin' off thet horse afore long, and we'll be bait for the green flies."

A shout from behind interrupted him, and we twisted about towards the stage. A back wheel was down in a deep mudhole, and the coach was tilted crazily; several sacks of grain had fallen off the top and burst on the ground.

Loping back, I looked up at Sam Goodson on the box. "Is

there an axe anywheres on the stage?" I asked him. "I'll be needin' a long pole to pry the wheel outta that hole."

"Back in the boot," he replied. "I'll get it, McCowan. I know just where it is."

"You stay right where you are," I told him. "Keep an eye peeled for Injuns." He nodded, and I handed him my reins.

"You git ready to shove them horses into their collars; I mean *shove*," I told Ada as I climbed down. "The timing's a lot more important than anything else. We'll git the stage to rockin', then give it a boost as you whip up the teams."

Taken me no more'n three minutes to cut down a strong and slender willow mebbe eight inches through. I trimmed it to a pole about twenty feet long and set it in under the axle.

"Garth! You ain't no good on the ground, so you'n Goodson can keep watch. Ben! Winters! Come on out here and give us a hand! You, too, Rousseau! We need your beef on this pry."

Brooke was already on the ground and hanging on. With a few tentative moves, we started the coach to rocking; slung on the long, leather thoroughbraces, it lent itself easily to what I had in mind.

Chanting, I called out, "One ... two ... and three! A big heave! That's ..." Something brushed my ear, and automatically I swatted it, thinking it was a big moth or an insect of some kind. As the coach lurched forward and came free of mud, I lost my balance and fell sprawling. The peddler, Lou Winters, was under me, and as I got to my feet, I reached out a hand to help him rise. Then I realized that an arrow was almost through his neck, the feathered end deep in the flesh of his throat. His eyes wide in terror, he was clawing desperately at the protruding shaft, and a strangled squawk was his only sound.

Blood poured down over his hands as he tugged at the tip end, and the painted shaft bowed in a dripping arc. Then he stiffened, and his eyes rolled back, only the whites showing now. His heels beat a brief tattoo. He was dead!

A bullet struck the stage! I heard its passing and saw the jagged white streak in the red-painted panel. Another, then another, as the dull reports sounded in our ears.

Through the trees, I got a glimpse of two or three riders moving at a trot, and I saw a rifle lifted for another shot. Garth had his pistol out and was firing at the riders as I hauled mine free and sighted at an Indian on a pinto horse. I touched one off and saw him slump over the horse's neck.

Winter's shotgun was on the ground in front of me, and an Indian was riding down on the lead team as I snatched it up and let go the right barrel. He was swept off of the horse and bounced heavily on the ground, rolling to a stop beneath the horse's hoofs. Terrified, they reared high in the air and came down repeatedly on his body, smashing through his rib cage and crushing his skull.

"Ada!" I screamed. "Git down! Lay down in the boot!" A half-dozen more riders could be seen in the trees, and I let off a carefully aimed shot at one, knocking him backwards to the ground.

The firing was continuous now. Garth and the Englishman were riding at the Indians from two sides, both scoring hits at the same time. Out of the corner of my eye, I saw one of the paint-bedaubed bucks charging in, a broad-bladed hatchet raised in one fist and a feathered lance held low. My hammer fell on a spent round, and I hurled the useless gun into his face as the pony shouldered me to the ground.

The slippery body of the Indian landed on top of me as I rolled into the mudhole, and the flat of his hatchet smacked me a stunning blow on the side of my head. Desperately, the Indian's throat in one hand and the hatchet's handle in the other, I fought off the blackness that threatened. His free hand was clawing at my eyes, and I buried my face close into his chest, conscious of the acrid animal musk of his writhing body. My nails dug into the flesh of his neck as I put more pressure into my hold on his throat. Then I jerked my head away from his chest and smashed it into his face. His grip on the hatchet loosened, and I butted him again. Then again and again, until he went limp.

My right hand went back to the sheath on my belt, and the bright blade of my bowie flashed in the sun. With the left, I grabbed a handful of his greasy hair, and the keen edge of the knife cut through to the bone as I ripped at the scalp.

"Rush! Rush! What are you doing, Rush? No!" It was the horrified scream that brought me back. Ada was tugging, Chilton helping her, as they pulled me off the dead Injun.

"It's all over, Rush. One of 'em got away, but we killed the rest. C'mon, man. It's all over!" It was Ben Chilton, and he had a curious look on his face.

As I got to my feet, I looked up at Ada and saw what was almost revulsion in her eyes. My head was still spinning, a feeling of nausea in the pit of my stomach.

"How'd we make out?" I asked. "Anybody hurt besides the peddler?" My strength was coming back, and my legs were not trembling now. Rousseau, his black suit splashed with mud, handed me my revolver.

"Here, McCowan," he said. "You might need this again. I saw what happened and tried to help, but I'd shot my pistol empty. You're very lucky! I thought he had you for sure."

Tom Brooke rode up, with Garth close behind. He showed a deep scratch along one cheek but otherwise seemed okay. In one hand, he was carrying a brass-framed Winchester rifle, a nearly new one, with bright blue on the barrel and magazine tube. Over his shoulder were two canvas belts, loops filled with shiny, copper cartridges. Glancing at Garth, I saw more. Another identical rifle, and a belt filled with ammunition.

"Look!" Tom showed us the belt's buckle. It was stamped deeply with the letters E.M. "I say!" he exclaimed. "This *is* rather unusual, isn't it? Those beggars were better armed than any of us. With the exception of you, McCowan, you having that fine Henry rifle. Which," he went on, "I didn't see you using during our little billy-doo. Why not, Rush?"

I shook my head. "I'm 'fraid I never got a chance. We was tryin' to git this stage outta the mud when them Injuns hit us. As you can see, the Henry's still in the scabbard."

As we talked, I reloaded the Remington and was pleased as I saw others doing the same. Forgetting to reload got a lot of fellers killed back during the war. It was not hard to do. Forgetting, I mean. Man gets pretty excited in the heat of combat, and he makes lots of mistakes.

Why, I've seen rifles that fellers loaded three, or sometimes four, times. Watched one once as he put that gun up to his shoulder, pointed it, then brought it down. He never pulled the trigger! Then he taken out his flask, poured the charge down the muzzle, and rammed a Minié ball down on top. Brought the rifle up to his shoulder, pointed it, and again failed to squeeze that trigger! I'd stopped him when I saw him load for the third time. That barrel was half full and would have surely burst in his face!

My .44 Remington was a fine revolver! Sam Colt made some mistakes in his time. One of 'em was in not enclosing the cylinders of his revolvers in a solid frame. By that, meaning there was no strap over the cylinder joining the barrel to the frame. His guns were easy to clean 'cause you could just stick that barrel down in a bucket of hot, soapy water and work your brush up and down, same like a pump. But the darn guns would always shoot loose in time. Plus, they can never be used as a club when empty. Too fragile.

I traded for my Remington no more'n six months before we got into fighting the war. Pack peddler came on through our part of the Kentucky hill country one day, and he had him a half dozen of these. They were shiny new, and he asked cash money for them. No trades, he told me. I paid him no mind.

Now hard money was seldom seen around there, but maw had known right off how bad I wanted that gun. She watched us go through all the motions. Trading was a serious business to hill folk, and a feller didn't want to rush things. That peddler never let on he was even interested as I laid out a half-dozen coon skins, a fine cougar pelt, and a red stone pipe. I added a good Barlow knife, and he never even blinked an eye. Course, the knife had one busted blade, but the big one was still there, and it taken a good edge. Kept it, too. First time I'd shaved my face, I'd used that knife.

I taken a good look at him, and he was just a-staring off into the distance like he couldn't care less. He did reach down for the pipe, though, and taken a look at that carving. That pipe had come down from Minnesota way. Paw'd traded an old flintlock pistol for that pipe. Got it off a Chippewa; one of them Indians from up north. Even now I can remember the funny-looking moccasins that Injun was wearing. Had an odd-shaped toe, sort of puckered up. Paw told us boys that was what Chippewa meant in their tongue. "To pucker up."

That peddler was a hard man! Two prime marten skins and a big brass belt buckle went onto the pile, and he just sat there, shaking his head. I'd about given up when I thought of one more thing I had to trade.

I didn't really want to part with it, but I sure ached to own that revolver! I'd picked it up one day when paw taken us boys back into the woods and told us about our Choctawan ancestors. It was a perfect war point, made out of a clear quartz crystal. Like a jewel, it sparkled and glittered.

That finally made an impression! He perked up considerably when I taken it out of a little buckskin bag I'd had on a leather whang around my neck. Sort of weighed it up'n down in his palm. Held it up to the light and squinted at it for a minute. He frowned, then opened his mouth.

"You're gettin' close," he told me, solemn-faced.

Well, sir! I was about at my wit's end! I'd plumb run out

of trading stock and had nothing more to give. I was about ready to offer to fight him for it when maw spoke up.

"My son'll need one of them flasks," she said. We'd seen the powder flasks, and they were beauties! Formed out of an alloyed copper, they showed a man wearing a stovepipe hat with a rifle under his arm and a dog walking alongside. An adjustable charger was in the spout. I'd not even considered a flask. Figgered it was way out of my reach.

"Yep!" maw went on. "He'll be needin' a bullet mould; an iron one, not one of them brass contraptions. We had oughta have some caps, too. Two boxes of them, number 'leven caps. Wouldn't hurt none was you to throw in some bar lead. Four bars would be enough, I reckon." Arms akimbo, she stared at the peddler, who hadn't said a word.

"Well! Don't jest set there, man! Git 'em out! Be ye a tradin' man or what?" She reached down into her apron pocket and brought out something knotted in a handkerchief. I watched as she undid the knot and taken out a gold coin of considerable size. She waved it under his jaw.

"This here's Mexican gold," she told us. "Eight *escudos*, they called it, worth 'bout the same as our double eagle. I got this from your paw when he come back from that war with Mexico. You were only six years old, Rush, back in '47."

She turned to the peddler and handed him the coin. Waving at the plunder I'd piled up, she told him the coin would be his. "But I want my son to keep his quartz arrow. Means a good deal to him," she said. "He found that point when my man was still alive, and they shared in the finding. My man was a pure-blood Injun, and he knowed about these things."

So I'd gotten my Remington gun, and it'd served me well for eight years now. I carried it through the war years, a sight of time, believe me. Aside from replacing the nipples in the cylinder a time or two, it was still tight and shot dead on at two hundred yards. That solid frame was the reason for it holding up so well.

My eyes swept the fringe around the clearing as I poured a measure of powder into the last, empty chamber. With some care, I set a ball on top of the charge and cranked it down tight with the loading lever. Then caps went on all of the nipples, and I let the hammer down between two chambers.

This time, I had loaded all six! Like I said before, this was not a really safe practice, but I wanted that extra shot now just in case. Old man Remington put a notch in between the chambers on the cylinder's rear, and it was there for a reason. I'd never trusted 'em, though; that's why I'd leave that empty to ride the hammer on.

I felt that mebbe I should say something to Ada. The unbelieving look she'd had on her face warned me that I best square myself, and fast! From what she'd told us, her uncle hadn't tried to shelter her from the hard realities of life, and she hadn't flinched when killing had to be done. Rolling on the ground in a welter of blood and gore and hacking away at a man's hair, that was entirely different! The fact that I'd been caught up in the heat of battle, my blood running hot and primitive instincts coming to the fore, didn't excuse what I'd almost done.

Suddenly, she had seen me in a different light. Shooting the holdups was one thing. I could imagine what my expression must have been, face covered with the Injun's blood, my eyes glaring crazily, and my knife sawing away at his scalp. To tell the truth, I was some repelled my own self!

CHAPTER 10

$\bf{O}$N MY ORDERS, BROOKE AND CHILTON TAKEN Winter's body over to the coach and propped it in one corner of the rear seat, secured with a length of the cotton rope. I'd told Rousseau to help, but he refused to touch the corpse.

It was the Cherry Creek Kid who really raised a fuss. He didn't much want a dead man riding next to him and told me in no uncertain terms.

"At least tie a neckerchief over his face," he told me, a look of anger on his own. "Bad enough havin' to sit on the same seat, much less him starin' at me like thet. Don't we have someplace else we can store him? Like back there with the grain, in the rear boot. Ain't gonna make him no nevermind wherever you haul him. Won't anger his feelin's none, and I'd feel a sight better. Dead folks make me oneasy."

Winters had a scarf in his pocket, so Brooke'd used it to cover the face. I really didn't blame the Kid. Winters had a strained, horrified look and wasn't nice to see, but none of us wanted to leave the body behind. He deserved a decent burial at the fort, and that's what he would have. I toyed with the idea of asking the others to help me bury them dead Injuns, but decided against it. The families of them bucks, wherever they were, would probably just as rather we'd leave 'em where they fell. 'Sides, we were in a kind of hurry.

I'd washed up in the river as best I could. Got a clean shirt out of my saddlebags and put it on. Taken a spell to rinse the blood outta the one I'd worn, but it was worth it. Even now, with money in the bank, I was savin' of my clothes and footwear.

Brooke, Chilton, and Goodson were at the back of the stage coach when I walked my horse up from the river. Garth and the gambler, Rousseau, were coming in from the other side, my other bandit, Bowie Knott, trailing behind. I wondered where they'd been and why, but decided not to ask.

Goodson had one of the new Winchesters in his hands and

a shell belt over his shoulder. "Lookee here, McCowan. Got something to show you," he said.

As I drew up next to him, he handed up the rifle. "There on the frame," he told me. "Just ahead of the trigger guard is that same mark. The 'E.M.,' same as the buckle. I worked the run from San Antonio to San Diego up 'til two months ago, and we hauled some of these to El Paso last spring. I b'lieve that mark means *Estados Mexicanos*, and them guns was meant for the Mexican army. Beats me how they could show up here in Nebraska, seven hundred miles away, when they was s'pose to go over the border to Ciudad Juarez a day after we dropped 'em off. No, sir! Don't make no sense to me!"

I handed back the Winchester. "Not only makes sense, Sam; it also made some fellers a whole bunch of money. Injuns'll give most anything for guns like these, and somebody's taken advantage of that. We see this in Texas all the time. The Kiowas and Comanches are better armed than the U.S. Army."

Ada had edged up to the group, and I signed to her that I wanted to talk. She seemed some reluctant, but nodded. The rifle was being passed about, and nobody paid us no mind as we moved to the front of the coach, me leading the chestnut.

"I'm sorry you had to see what you did," I told her. "I was sure enough fightin' for my life with that feller, so's I sorta let my temper run away with me. It's the God's own truth, I never done nothin' like that before. Honest! You and me got somethin' betwix us that's worth savin' and will be saved if you'll just let it happen."

She looked up at me, then looked away. "I believe you, Rush. But I just don't know! If you could have seen yourself as I did then. You looked like a vicious animal, not one bit better than the savage you were fighting. I'm used to men fighting. My uncle's hired hands fought each other for the pure pleasure of fighting. Especially in the slack times, the winter months, when there wasn't much for them to do. Like Uncle Frank, I believed it was a healthy outlet, a way for them to 'blow off steam,' so to speak. I know you'd no alternative. If you hadn't killed that Indian, he'd have most certainly killed you." She shook her head sadly.

"It was the way you did it! Throttling him; his eyes all bulged out and his face turning black. Then . . ." she shuddered. "Then . . . your knife . . . Oh!" She turned away from me, and her shoulders shook as she sobbed quietly. "Please give me some time to think, Rush. I must have time! It's a bit too fresh in my mind right now. Please understand!"

What could I say to her? I sure enough hadn't planned to scalp that Injun; it had just been something cooked up in my anger and fear. I was certain sure that I loved this girl, but I resented having to apologize and defend what I'd done.

Her comparing the rough-and-tumble antics of her uncle's hired help with my fight for life against a wild Injun in a way was comical. No! It wasn't! It was just plain ignorance and narrow-mindedness!

Whoa up, Rush McCowan! You can't love her very much, not if you can think those things about her! Which brings me to what I'm beginning to wonder about. Do I really love this beautiful girl, or am I just attracted to her beauty? After all, I'd been crazy about Julia, too, and I'd gotten over it pretty easily. Mebbe I was simply in love with the idea of being in love?

Yes, sir! That *could* be my problem, all right. Outwardly, I was a happy-go-lucky feller, and laughing come easy to me. But maw had teached us to take serious things serious. The loving of a woman for me was a real serious business and should end in marriage, a home, and children. Mebbe it had not oughta be that way every time. I'd only been acquainted with two beautiful women in my life; been real close, I mean, and I'd fallen in love with both of them. Or had I?

Trouble was, I didn't have that many chances to meet with pretty women. Or any women, for that matter, and mebbe that was my problem. I was so anxious that I mistook attraction for genuine affection. Why, I'd known some fellers that had sparked a different girl every day of the week; leastwise to hear 'em talk, they had, and they looked on it as they would shaving their face. Just something that had to be done. It had always seemed to me like that was wrong; not necesarily sinful, but not the right way to be treating a good woman.

Well! Right now I had better things to worry about. We had best git on our way, and quick like, I figgered. There'd been something nagging at me, and now it came out. That one Injun that'd got plumb away! Chances are he'd be back, and real soon, and it was a hidebound cinch he wouldn't be all by his lone self. Our tracks were plain as a printed page, a thing we couldn't help. The stage was heavy, and the wheels sank deep into the sandy soil of the river bottoms.

I patted Ada on her shoulder. "We got to git movin', I know. We can talk this all out later, Ada. Right now, forget everything else and just concentrate on drivin' horses. C'mon, I'll give you a boost up into the box, and then git a little action out of the rest of this bunch."

Me and Garth scouted up ahead like before. I'd parceled out them two new Winchesters to him and Rousseau so's we'd have firepower in the hands of them as knew how to use 'em. Chilton had decided to chance riding a horse this time, and he picked out one of the three Injun ponies we'd managed to capture. Two had stood ground-hitched, their riders on the sand, dead. The other had run through our party, and my saddle mate, Garth, had grabbed his war bridle. It was a lot bigger'n most Injun mounts; a tall, Roman-nosed roan with a deep chest and massive shoulders. Strangely enough, he accepted Ben on his back without much argument.

It made me wonder, so I'd taken a look. Up under a twist of the rawhide bridle, I found a small jaw brand; the "CV" of Charley Goodnight, a pretty well known rancher in Texas.

I'd never met Mr. Goodnight, but I'd heard a whole lot about him. Lancelot Gilkie, my cook on that drive last year, had worked for Goodnight in the past. From what he'd said, I'd gotten the idea that Goodnight would not take kindly to someone riding a horse with his brand on it. As a matter of fact, he'd been known to decorate nearby trees with fellers riding his horses or driving his stock without permission.

Now all this was turning into quite a riddle, but I surely didn't have the time or inclination to fool around, at least not right now. But it was a puzzler! Northern Injun bucks with Texas guns and a Texas horse, and all this way up in Nebraska! We'd report it to the military at Kearny.

Chilton had the Triplett & Scott rifle and seemed trusting of it, so I put him and Rousseau out as wide flankers on either side. Bowie Knott and Tom Brooke covered the rear of the coach with orders to stick with it no matter what happened to the rest of us.

The going was getting some easier. The Little Blue, some time back, had apparently flooded over its banks, and now a fairly wide path lay on both sides of the river, right up to the cut bank where the river had gouged out a new bed. Ada was able to move the stage along at a good clip, and me and Garth had to trot them horses right smartly to keep ahead.

It was coming on to midday when I called a halt so's a fresh set of teams could be hitched to the coach. I figgered some hot coffee would taste good to everybody, and I asked Bowie

Knott to get a small fire started. We'd pulled up close to the cut bank, and some good-sized cottonwoods overhung at that point. The smoke from the fire would be filtered up through the branches and hopefully not be seen.

Grayson's missus had included some corn dodgers in those food supplies she'd given us. Goodson broke 'em out, and I had him distribute them around to those who needed them. A corn dodger's a lasting thing. They stick to your ribs and stay with you for some time. But I'd found them best just shortly after they were baked. Or boiled or fried, as your taste fancied. Didn't take long for them to get so goldurn hard you had to bust 'em with a hammer to eat 'em. These, having been baked only last night, were soft and crumbly. I ate two and stuck another two in my saddlebags for later.

As we kicked dirt over the fire and got ready to pull on out of there, I noticed that Rousseau had once more gotten a ways off from the camp and had Garth and Knott in conversation. As I watched, he patted Bowie on the back and reached out to shake Garth's hand. I had no idea what they'd had to talk about, but I'd bet hard money Rousseau was up to no good. He was a strange man, but easy to read; a loner, he'd never really trust anyone and, in turn, could not be trusted himself! I made a mental note to sound out Garth first chance I got. Sure! Red Garth was an outlaw, but he'd never go back on his word or cheat somebody who trusted him.

Just as we were leaving, Goodson spotted a thin column of smoke rising up to the west of us and called our attention to it. Looking at my watch, I saw we'd been on the move for almost three hours. That would put us about due east of the stage station at Liberty Farm. Poor devils! They had held out as long as they could, I guessed. There was nothing we could do to help them except tell the military at Kearny.

Hopefully, at least for our sakes, the lone Injun survivor of our recent battle would have trouble dragging any of that bunch away from the looting of the station. Leastways, not right away. Once they'd finished there, they'd be after us for sure! 'Specially with us having a young woman, over twenty head of horses, and a whole lot of late-model guns.

Garth had been very quiet. As we rode along, he kept a close watch on his half of the territory ahead but seemed a touch reluctant to look me in the face. I knew he must have something on his mind but couldn't think of a way to begin. I decided to sorta "prime" the pump, so to speak. "The

Injuns must have finally overrun Liberty Farm," I said. "We more'n likely can expect 'em whoopin' and hollerin' after us next soon's they finish up over there."

"Yeah!" he replied. "Depends . . . If any of them folks was left alive, them red devils'll stay long enough to make them wish they was dead. Poor thing to wish on anybody, but it'd mean we'd mebbe hold onto our hair if they was to hang and rattle there for a spell longer." He turned in the saddle and looked at me square in the eye.

"You got yourself more to worry about than jest them red Injuns," he told me. "There's a feller right here who'd be happy to lift your scalp or stretch your peltry on a willow frame. I reckon you got an idea who I'm talkin' about."

I nodded. "Rousseau!" I told him grimly. "But why? I ain't never laid eyes on him before this trip. Surely the little scuffle we had yesterday ain't got him that riled?"

Garth shifted in the saddle. "Durned leg of mine won't quit achin'! Don't know why I'm feelin' kindly towards you after you pluggin' me this way. Reckon it could be because you taken our word and trusted us boys with our guns. Even so, I'm servin' notice here and now! I got no intention of spending ten years of my young life locked up in some state pen somewheres. Ruther be dead than to be locked away!

"As for you wondering why thet snake wants you dead. I don't know, but I got me a suspicion. His shoulder rig was made by a feller named Varga, in El Paso, and it's durn near new! I'd say thet Mister Rousseau was *in* El Paso, and not a long time back. 'Bout the same time as them Winchesters.

"Ben Varga made this belt'n holster for me, and his border stamping is different from any other saddler. Notice the way he joins the tails of them chain stamps." He lifted his holster and showed me the elaborate decoration.

"Rousseau's is 'xactly the same's mine. Now there surely is a darkie in the woodpile somewheres. Yessir! I'd be willin' to swear thet hombre knows how them guns and Goodnight's hoss wound up here in Nebraska. Said he was on his way to Cheyenne, didn't he? Said he had to be there soon's possible. Mebbe he has him a partner and they plan to meet there and divvy up their profits? Hell, McCowan. I got no rock-hard proof, but I can read sign pretty good. Thet feller's as crooked as a dog's hind laig, and I'd bet cash money he's tied into them guns somehow!"

"What did he want you fellers to do?" I asked him. "Help him kill me or just hold off the others while he done it?"

He nodded affirmatively. "Yep! You got it! Told us we should stand for him when he braces you. Jest make sure it went down without them others backin' you. Said he'd start hoorahin' you so's to git your mad up and then it wouldn't look bad to the others. He'd jest be defendin' hisself.

"Figgered he could talk them others into leavin' thet old coach behind," he continued. "He'd take the girl along with him and tell the others it was every man for hisself; so's me'n my pards could go anywhere we pleased. Nobody would be tryin' to hang onto us because they'd be too busy trying to save their own skins." He paused and rubbed his bad leg.

"Hard to understand why he picked on us," he went on. "I reckon it was 'cause he had nobody else to ask. Got hisself a real short memory, hasn't he? Thet coyote forgits he was the one who stomped on the Kid's hand! Why Cherry Creek'n me go way back together! We rode line together down there in Nueces, and we been *compañeros* since who laid the chunk! So you jest play 'em as you see 'em, and we'll back you."

"I 'preciate that, Red," I told him. "We'll let him make the first move. I ain't yearnin' to kill nobody right now on account I already got Miss Ada mad at me for what I done to that wild Injun. She figgers I'm some sort of animal."

Garth glanced over at me from under his hat brim, and the corners of his mouth turned up in a grin. "Seen you was a mite put down," he said. "Me, I give up tryin' to read the signs of women a long time ago. Seems like a feller's got no chance with a good woman. I'm skeered of 'em myself!

"Minds me of a time, down on the Brazos—" He broke off suddenly. Ahead of us was a tight bend to the east with a heavy growth of willow and dogwood trees. A large flock of birds had risen suddenly, their raucous cries echoing across the river channel.

Wheeling, we streaked back to the stage, gesturing at Ada to pull closer to the cut bank. I waved in Chilton and Rousseau, and they rode in to where the stage halted, up against the overhanging bluff.

"Me'n Red figger that we're in for some trouble," I said. "Something scared hell outta a bunch of birds up there near the bend. No way we can flank 'em with these bluffs pinchin' us in, so we'll just ride on up there and see what happens. Who wants to ride with me?"

Seemed like everybody's hand went up, but I'd had already figgered who I wanted along with me. It was almost like my plans were being worked out in advance. If there was to be a showdown, I wanted it on my own terms.

Automatically, I checked the loads in my Henry and loosened the Remington in its holster, flipping off the thong I kept over the hammer.

"You ready?" I asked Rousseau. He nodded, and we started towards the bend, riding about twenty feet apart. It was an unusually warm day, but I felt an icy chill go down my back, and the hairs bristled on my neck.

We were really exposed out there, but I was hoping those Injuns, or whatever was hiding in the trees, would hold off. It made sense! Was I thinking to ambush a bunch of folks, I would let the scouts get in close before I did anything. A man can be killed without using a gun, and it would be some kind of advantage if the stage passengers could be led into the belief that the scouts had made it through all right.

Once, during the war, I'd gotten myself out of a spot by pretending I was a scout for a larger force. Actually, that Yankee infantry had let me go by scot-free, thinking that a full company, or more, was coming along behind me. I'd just made all the motions that a regular scout would have made.

We'd been moving in at a fast, running walk but now that seemed to slow. "Kick that critter into a lope," I hollered at Rousseau. "Let's git it over with!"

With no more'n a hundred yards to go, the thunderous roar of a big-bore rifle bellowed in the stillness, and I watched Rousseau's hat go sailing. We reined up, right sudden!

A harsh voice cried out. "Jest you hold it right now! This here's a Buffalo Sharps, and the next one'll be in your brisket! This close, ain't no way I can miss!"

That wasn't no Injun! Matter of fact, sounded sorta like a woman's voice, but I couldn't be sure. One thing for certain! We were well in range no matter if we did try to run from the hidden rifleman. He, or she, would have us before we'd gotten any distance at all.

I taken a chance. "Yes, ma'am," I hollered back. "We're friendly, so you can put down that cannon you got there. A stage is right behind us, and we've a woman along, so you've got you no worries. We don't plan you no harm, honest!"

"Jest you keep them hands on them saddle horns and come a bit closer. That's it! Little mite closer. Now git off them horses and lay flat to the ground. Keep them hands in plain sight now! I can part your hair with this Sharps."

"No, ma'am," I called back. "You wait just a dern minute! We're in hostile country, and them Injuns is all around. If you want to come on outta them trees and be friends, that's just fine! But we ain't gonna crawl around on our hands and knees like a couple of mangy coyotes! If you're gonna kill me'n my friend here, you'd best git on with it!"

"Well . . . Aw right, honey boy," the answer came back. "I believe you. Easy to see you ain't Injuns, and you sound as if you're tellin' the gospel truth. I got troubles and can sure use some help. Got me a hurt man in here, and he's in bad shape. Bleedin' somethin' awful, and I can't do nothin' to git it stopped. Stay on them horses if you want, but by God, c'mon in here! C'mon! Won't shoot again, I promise. I swear on my dead momma's grave. Listen . . . I'm lettin' down the hammer on this here Sharps and layin' it down. There!"

In the still air, the sound of a hammer being lowered was plain to hear. I nudged the chestnut and pushed on through the trees, Rousseau close behind me.

Well, sir! You could have knocked me down with a blade of bunch grass. A mountainous fat woman was standing there at the edge of a small clearing. Near her feet was the Sharps and a slight figure covered with a blanket. Lank, bleached hair straggled down over the low-cut bodice of a filthy red dress that was wet and muddy to the knees. Apparently, she had forded the Little Blue and must have carried her friend on her back. Right now a good bit of her threatened to overflow the bodice, and the rest jiggled as she bent down.

"This here's Connie," she said, fussing with the blanket. "Conrad Snelling . . . He's been shot up some. Saved my life, he did! Rousted me out when them Injuns hit the station . . . Pore little critter! He taken lead that was aimed right at me. Please! Help me to save him! I'll give you . . . Ungh!"

From behind me, Rousseau's Colt boomed, and I saw crimson blossom at the base of her throat; her head jerked back, and her eyes widened in disbelief as she collapsed in a heap on the blanket-covered figure. Shocked and mad clean through, I whirled to face the gambler, who stood there smiling, the smoking gun in his fist.

"Why?" I shouted. "Why'd you want to do that? You crazy or something?" I couldn't believe he'd shot down a helpless woman, on her knees, begging us to help her!

He was grinning as he eared back the hammer of his Colt and sighted down the barrel at me. Desperately, I lunged at him, clawing at his extended arm! Something hit me a hammer blow above my right eye, and I felt myself falling. Noise filled my ears, and bright lights flashed as I felt a searing pain in my head. Like far away, I seemed to hear voices calling and heard the spiteful "pop" of a small-bore gun.

Rousseau cursed, and again his navy boomed. If I was hit again, I didn't feel it. I heard someone groan and another pop from the little gun. Then a long, drawn-out sigh and a wheezing, bubbling intake of breath; then silence.

Another loud explosion, and someone yelling. What was Rousseau's idea? Sure, he wanted me dead, but why an innocent woman? My mouth was gritty with sand, and I tried hard to spit it out, but couldn't bring up any saliva. I could hear somebody breathing awful hard; then realized it was me making all that noise. Gasping, I strained to get up off the ground and finally got part way, my head spinning.

On my hands and knees, my arms gave way, and I fell flat, my face grinding into the coarse sand. Damn! Rolling over, I rubbed my eyes with my shirt-sleeve. If I could just see, then I'd know what was going on! Something warm was running down my face, and it felt like a red-hot brand had been held against my head! The pain had me dizzy and sick, and I felt so dern helpless! Where was everybody? Had to hear shots!

With my ear close to the ground, I could hear horses running and coming closer. Then they were right there, sand showering over me as one slid to a stop practically on top of me. Somebody knelt and slid an arm around my shoulders, pulling me into a sitting position there on the ground.

"Take it easy, Rush. You've been shot, but you'll be all right now. Easy, now. I'm jest tryin' to help. Here, take a swig of this water. That's enough. Let me see if some of this here blood'll wash off." I felt the cool water running down my face and a cloth dabbing at my eyes. Boy! I could feel my eyelids loosening as the blood was washed away.

I opened my eyes and saw Red Garth's freckled face bending close to mine. "Yeah!" he said. "It's me, all right."

"Rousseau!" I told him. "It was Rousseau. He shot right smack into her! It was like he was a crazy man! Where'd he run to, anyway? We gotta catch him! He's a damn killer! I don't know what got into him? Gunned down the woman 'thout no warnin'! His brains must be addled or somethin'! She'd shot his hat off to warn us back, but that sure didn't give him no call to kill her! Help me up, Red. We're gonna find that yaller dog and make him wish he'd never been borned!"

"Rousseau's dead, Rush. He's been holed three times. We got us three dead folks here, and we'd best be figgerin' on clearin' out of here and fast. Them Injuns'll be follerin' them gunshots and be on us like flies on cow platters. You want to try'n stand up? Here! Lemme give you a hand."

With Garth's help, I made it to my feet. My head was not all that clear as yet, but I could see again, and that sure made some difference! Knott had rolled me a smoke, and that tasted pretty good. He handed me my Remington after wiping off the sand. I had no recollection of drawing it, so mebbe it had just fallen out of the holster. After checking loads and caps, I put it back.

Garth gave me another drink from his canteen and tied my neckerchief around my forehead. Gingerly, I fitted my Texas hat down over it and wiped the blood off my face as best I could with my shirt tail.

"I ain't leavin' them two here for the Injuns," I declared. "Rousseau, I couldn't care less, but them two others is goin' along with us. We ain't got time to bury 'em." Then I got to thinking. Who had shot who? Didn't make much of a difference now, but I was curious to know, so I asked.

"Well, Rousseau plugged the woman, and then he drew down on you. This little feller, in the blankets, had him a Reid knuckle duster. You know, one of them little seven-shot .22 derringers.

"We could hear the shots, of course, so it ain't hard for us to figger. The little man shot Rousseau in the face. It wasn't a killin' wound, but it hit him in the cheekbone. Then Rousseau fired into him with his navy Colt. Next shot made little noise, so that was the second shot from the Reid. It hit Rousseau in the eye and killed him dead.

"There was one more shot from Rousseau's Colt, but it wasn't fired by him. When we got here, we found this little feller laying up against Rousseau with the navy in his hand. He'd stuck that navy in the gambler's mouth and touched her off. You wouldn't recognize him, Rush. The little feller's dead, of course. Rousseau's shot hit him in the chest, but he was already shot up pretty bad. Had two arrows in him, too. A real man, that little feller!"

CHAPTER 11

§§§

GARTH AND TOM BROOKE WERE SCOUTING AHEAD of the stage, my head not quite up to trotting a horse. Goodson had given up his seat on the box and was lying on top, while I rode the messenger's place.

We'd shoveled a little sand over the gambler, not wanting the Indians to find him right off, and the bodies of the two others were on the floor of the coach. The Kid hadn't raised much of a fuss this time, but he did insist that they be wrapped in blankets and laid on the floor. Between middle and front seats, they were more or less out of his sight.

Not much had been said by either of us in the two hours since we'd left the site of the shooting. Ada had busted in there all ready to chew me up one side and down the other. But shock and uncertainty had showed in her expression the moment she saw the dead scattered around and me standing in there with blood all over my shirt. Right now I wanted to say I understood, but I was too proud, I reckon. Figgered she'd get around to saying something once she was ready. I snuck a look at her out of the corner of my eye. She was a real beautiful girl; there was no doubt of that.

Right now she was sitting there relaxed, the lines from all six horses lying between her fingers. Every now'n then she'd tighten up on one or slack off on a couple. Her arms see sawed back and forth in easy rhythm to the trot cadence of the teams, and her right foot rested lightly on the brake lever. The broad behinds of the wheelers bobbed up'n down directly in front of us, and now and then she'd just barely touch that off-wheeler's rump with the whip she kept tucked under the curve of her right thumb.

I was running out of patience. "Nice day," I said, the words barely above a whisper. She nodded and smiled.

"I hear old Ulysses Grant is runnin' for president ag'in a Democrat. Horatio Seymour's his name. Reckon he'll win?"

She shrugged, her eyebrows lifted. "One's got as good an opportunity as the other," she replied.

Somewhat encouraged, I continued. "The Congress passed an amendment to the Constitution here recently. Means that former slaves now have citizenship rights. I read it in the Leavenworth *Daily Conservative*. It's the Fourteenth Amendment."

"That's nice," she said. "I'm glad for them."

"Did you know that Japan has a brand-new emperor?" I asked. "Feller named Mutsuhito. First time in seven hundred years they ain't had a whole bunch of 'warlords,' as they called 'em, a runnin' bits and pieces of their country. Reckon he's sort of like our president, only he don't have to run for office. Just gets him together a whole lot of soldiers and wins the war. That makes him the top dog no matter what."

She looked over at me. "I'll bet you read all about it in that Leavenworth newspaper, didn't you?"

I grinned. "No, ma'am. It was the Atchison *Free Press*. I did read it in the lobby of the National Hotel, though, and it's *in* Leavenworth, so you're not all wrong."

Ada laughed, and I joined in. "You're incorrigible, do you know that?" she said. "But I can't stay mad at you. By the way," she said, her voice real serious, "how badly were you hurt? I was afraid to look, with all that blood running down your face."

"Outside of a headache, I'm just fine," I told her. "It's just a graze, but it sure knocked me kickin'! My maw said I was born to hang, and I reckon she was right. Course, she'd just seen me runned over by an eight hundred pound sow at the time; a real mad old sow 'cause I'd roped me one of her piglets. I come out of that with nothin' more'n scratches and bruises."

"I would imagine you've had even more narrow escapes. In the war, for instance. Did you stand for the Union, or were you one of those Johnny Rebs we heard so much about?"

"I'm 'fraid I was one of them rebs, Ada. Me'n my brother was cavalry! Rode with Vaughn's Brigade and almost won the War single-handed. If'n General Lee hadn't surrendered, we'd still be out there doin' our best for old Dixie!"

"We really don't know much about each other, do we, Rush? I'm an Ohio girl, born and bred. My father ran a livery and short-line stage out of Wooster. Actually, he built it up until he had stages running out about forty miles in almost every direction. We had five county seats within that forty miles and lots of smaller towns in between. Uncle Frank was the boss driver until papa died."

"How come you'n Frank came out here to the wild west?" I was curious to learn why she'd left what sounded like a going business to take a long chance on starting fresh.

Ada grimaced. "Dad was having problems with rival outfits that wanted the whole pie. As long as he was still in charge, they were afraid to move in. When he died, the line died with him. Some of the drivers quit, not wanting a girl for a boss. Others were persuaded to leave. One was killed from ambush. Shot right off of the box. The local sheriff and the district judge were both paid to look the other way. One deputy tried to help, and they ran him out of town."

"But you had your uncle there! Couldn't he ramrod a line like that? Seem's like a pretty tough old codger to me! I figgered he'd just naturally rear up on his hind legs, knock down anybody in his way, and tell the rest to cut bait."

"Oh, he tried, but Uncle Frank was never cut out to be an owner. Driver . . . Sure! One of the best! But he couldn't, or wouldn't be boss! I told him I'd handle all of the paperwork. Arrange all the contracts and waybills. Even do all of the hiring and firing. No . . . One by one, we lost all of our steady customers. Some were threatened, I guess. I had no way to promise them protection. No one to stand up there with me and back up my promises." She paused, and her eyes were gazing far beyond the lead team.

"I needed a fighter, Rush! Someone like you, who'd back down from no man! Someone . . ." She looked away for a brief moment. "Someone who knew guns and wasn't hesitant about using them. There! I've said it!" She turned and looked squarely into my eyes.

"Forgive me for being such a ninny back there. That man was trying to kill you. The Indian, I mean. What you meant to do is immaterial. You didn't do it even though you had every right to do whatever was necessary to save your life."

I squirmed uneasily. "Now, Ada," I began. "What we best do is to forgit all about that there scramble with the Injun. Sure! I was fightin' for my life, all right, but it was wrong to try'n scalp that feller. I'm sorry you had to see it, and I'd give most anything if it had never happened that way. I was mad! And believe me, I was scared! But I want you to believe me when I say that I never did anything like that before, and I never will again. Let's talk about what we're gonna do when this here trip comes to an end.

"Say!" I exclaimed. "Have you ever been to Chicago? I never have, but my old partner Charley Canfield's sure been after me to visit there. He's in the cattle sales business, and he knows all the fancy places. How about we ride on up in the steam cars and have us a time? See all the sights a body can find and eat in some of them French restaurants. I would be a perfect gentleman; you can be sure of that. And who knows, you may even git to likin' me."

She smiled. "I know you'd be a gentleman, Rush, and we probably would have a grand time. But I've got a business, and I have responsibilities. I can't just run off and hope it'll still be here when we got back." She put her hand on my arm.

"It's even more important now. With Indians burning all my stations and killing my employees, I may have to more or less start from scratch. It means constructing new way stations, buying horses, and hiring new personnel. All this has to cost money, and I may have to borrow from the bank."

"Heck!" I told her. "I got money if that's all you'll be needin'. I got me an account in Kansas City, and there's my share of last year's herd money. All I gotta do is wire to my brother back there in Texas. Must be twenty thousand I can do with as I please! It can git here in a week."

I was surprised to see tears in her eyes. She looked for something to dry them with, gave up, and taken a quick swipe with her coat sleeve.

"Turn coming up," she muttered. "Give me a minute or two to make it. It's going to be a tight squeeze."

Her foot pressed down on the brake lever ever so slightly, and I could hear a faint rasping noise. I seen the off leader's ears prick up and his head trying to turn, while a noticeable difference showed in his stride. It was like he'd anticipated the coming turn and was all ready for it. When I mentioned this to Ada, she just grinned.

Another light bit of pressure on the brake and now both leaders had their ears up, and Ada had the lines drawn a bit tighter. She reached down and tapped the off wheeler with the tip of her whip, and he shoved tighter into the collar.

Now we were at the turn, a tight one, with a sandy wash a mere foot or so from the left wheels. Smoothly, the leaders made the turn, with the swings and wheelers streaming on around the curve at just the right moment. Like she'd said earlier, it was the same as soldiers executing column right.

Once around the turn, Ada eased pressure on the brake as the lines slackened in her hands. It was a beautiful sight and one not easily forgotten. A real precision move!

Easing back in her seat, she glanced at me, then said her piece. "I couldn't take money from you, Rush. Especially after what was said between us out on the prairie. If it's supposed to happen...If we *are* able to spend our lives together, then I want to come to you on equal terms. I don't want money involved in any way. Can you understand, Rush?"

"Sure! Sure, Ada! Well, don't you worry none. We're not gonna git caught by them Injuns. We'll make it through; you just believe old Uncle Rush. No more'n fifteen minutes ago, we passed a good-sized creek drainin' into the Little Blue. That's gotta be Thirty-two-Mile Creek, and it's only thirty-five or so miles from Fort Kearny. At the rate you're pushin' these horses, we could make it easy in four or five hours. As for building new stations and the like, I hope you won't mind a man lendin' a hand. I ain't exactly a finish carpenter, but I'm good at choppin' down trees and buildin' cabins. Don't you worry your pretty little head. We'll git them horses.

"Which reminds me, Ada. It's about time to change teams. See that pair of cottonwoods up ahead? Pull in close so's there'll be some shade while you wait."

She nodded, and moments later, we were stripping the harness off and transferring it to fairly fresh horses. I sent Garth and Tom Brooke out for a little look-see. To check a bit and make sure we were alone out there. They came back all smiles with the words we all wanted to hear.

"Ain't a soul around, McCowan," Garth reported. "What say we brew a pot of coffee. Sure would taste good about now!"

I agreed and set about starting a hat-sized fire. Knott brought me some small dry twigs, and we sat there a moment, waiting for the fire to catch. Bowie had something he wanted to say and wasted no time getting to the point.

"I been talkin' with Garth and the Kid, and we decided a spell in the pen might not hurt nobody, but it sure wouldn't do 'em no good. So...I'm askin' you nice if you're still bound and determined to turn us over to them sojers at Fort Kearny. Sure! We shot the old man, but we wouldn't of done thet if he hadn't tried to draw down on us. Wait a minute, now!" He held up his hand.

"Let me finish, McCowan! I ain't sayin' thet we're not a mite deservin' of punishment. We did try to hold up a stage company coach, but all we got was knocked around and gunned down for our trouble. Now you can believe this or not. I ain't never done nothin' like this before, nor have the Kid or Garth. We're jest three cowboys that made a mistake. A bad mistake thet could happen to most anybody! You know... Like the Book says, about castin' thet first stone...

"So... I'm askin' you to see if you can't talk thet lady into fergittin' what happened. We'll stick tighter'n burrs 'til we git this stage to the fort. Then we're gonna vamos. Myself, I'd jest as soon there wasn't no posters doggin' us, but we're gonna skeedaddle however the stick floats. All I got to say, Mc-Cowan." He hung his head and stirred a stick in the fire.

There wasn't much I could say. They had their guns back, and we had enough to worry about without having to fight amongst ourselves.

"I'll do what I can," I told him. "That don't mean you'd be ridin' away from this trouble scot-free. You ain't just perched on the top of my list, neither. I didn't hire on to mollycoddle a bunch of down-at-the-heels cowpokes that woke up broke and went on the owl hoot to git their *dinero* back.

"Now! This lady's gonna be needin' a lot of help gittin' her stage line back in business. Injuns have burned down her stations and run off her stock. Killed some of her tenders, too, and some cut and run. Now mebbe, just mebbe, she'd see her way clear to lettin' you'n your pards work off what you owe her. If she will, I'll forgit what happened."

Knott looked up and added a few wrinkles to his brow. "I don't understand," he said. "What're you talkin' about? A job, you mean? You sayin' she might let us work for her? I reckon you must be crazier'n me, McCowan! Give us a chance after we held up her first stage run? Hell, man! I ain't a feller thet thinks much of doin' nothin' less'n it's off of the back of a hoss, but I'll bust my gut for her if'n she'd give me a chance. Garth and the Kid'll feel the same. You do what you can, and we'll play our string on the square."

I nodded and put the coffee on to boil. Now was as good a time as any, I figgered, so I taken Ada off to one side to explain the situation. I wasn't too surprised when she was only too happy to agree. After all, she needed the men, and these would be handy and probably some cheaper.

"Of course you'll have to pay 'em something," I said as we walked along together. "A top hand gits around forty and found right now, but they'd be happy with a dollar a day."

"I'll do it!" she replied enthusiastically. "Might have some argument from Uncle Frank, but I can handle him. Rush! You're a wonder! Do you know that? You have a rare ability to turn misfortune into something beneficial. Why, I'd bet if you were struck by lightning, you'd look up, say thanks a whole lot, and use it to start a fire."

We both laughed, and she squeezed my hand. I was feeling pretty good right now. Seemed like we might make the fort without further trouble from the Injuns, and this grand girl was including me in her future.

"Coffee should be ready 'bout now," I told her. "I could sure use a cup. I feel pretty good, and my head's quit hurtin', so I'll git back on my horse. C'mon girl! We got the whole dern world by the tail, and we're on a downhill pull!"

CHAPTER 12

M E'N GARTH WERE BACK ON POINT, WHILE TOM
Brooke trailed a ways behind the coach. With Bowie Knott on
the right flank and my friendly enemy Ben Chilton on the left,
I felt fairly secure from any surprise attack from the Indians.

"Don't reckon as I've ever seen Fort Kearny." Garth was
just making conversation, I guessed. Probably he was waiting
for me to say something about my talk with Knott.

"Yep!" he went on. "I come close one time, coupla years
back, when them Sioux broke off the reservation. Local lawman
swore a few of us in as special deputies, and we trailed one
bunch within ten miles of the fort before we ketched up with
'em. How does it lie, and is there a town close by?"

"It's just south of the Platte River crossing," I answered
back. "As for a town, there's a conglomeration of shacks and
saloons close by. Folks there call it Doby Town."

Red looked over and grinned. "I can imagine what they'd
have to offer in a place like thet. A good one to stay out of
for fellers like me'n my friends. 'Specially with empty pockets.
Say!" His grin faded, and his expression was more serious. He
hunched that leg again and looked over at me.

"What did the little lady think of your proposition? Are we
still jail bait, or is she gonna let us work it out?"

I explained Ada's reaction to what I'd suggested, and the
grin came right back! This time, from ear to ear. "Well, I
declare!" he burst out. "You're all right, McCowan, in spite
of what folks say about you. Ha! Ha! Ha! I was only funnin'
with you, Rush. Well, I'll be derned! Wait'll Bowie and the
Kid hear about this!" He reached out his hand. "Go ahead!
Shoot me in the other laig," he said. "It'd be worth it!"

We shaken hands, and I was sorta embarrassed. After all,
it was Ada deserved any credit that was due. I glanced up and
taken a look at the sky.

107

"Gonna be dark before long," I observed. "Suns' gittin' mighty low, and there ain't gonna be much twilight in these bottoms. Them bluffs are castin' long shadows already. We can figger on slowin' down some, and we may have to hole up 'til daybreak. I ain't none too happy 'bout that."

Garth nodded in agreement. "Yeah!" he replied. "I don't care much for stumblin' around in the dark, 'specially with them hostiles all around us. I'm s'prised we've got by this long without them swarmin' all over us. Could be they had themselves a time at Liberty Farm. Mebbe there was enough likker there to git 'em all drunk. Ain't much an Injun can do when he's full of whiskey. They just can't handle that, or so I've heard tell." He smiled abashedly.

"Reckon thet takes in a lot of territory. Myself, I jest ain't wu'th shucks when I been drinkin'. Never could drink jest one glass long's I had money to buy more. Mebbe thet means I'm part Injun, though I doubt it, with this red hair and all. My paw was a wanderin' man, or so I've been told.

"Never knew either one of 'em. My paw or my maw. First recollection I got was an orphanage down in St. Louie. I come there in a basket with the name Garth pinned onto my britches. I runned off from there when I was 'bout twelve, near as they could figger. Stowed away on a keel boat goin' down the Mississippi to New Orleans.

"They found me when I got so dern hungry I had to crawl outta my hidee hole. One feller was all for givin' me a raw switchin' and tossin' me over the side. I settled his hash right off by shovin' him into the river.

"Anyways, they let me stay and work my way down river. I got real friendly with one boatman who said he'd known of a feller named Garth. Said he looked a good deal like I did, with red hair'n all. He's the one told me about the wanderin' part. The Garth he knew was a mountain man who spent his summers in St. Louie and sure did like the ladies.

"I paid off with 'leven dollars in hard cash and got me a job on the docks down there. You know, loadin' bales and unloadin' crates. Was mostly cotton goin' on outta that port. Sometimes I made me some extra money runnin' errands for sailors, like gittin' 'em whiskey or whatever they'd be wantin', and that's when I got started drinkin' likker.

"I worked around there for nigh on to a year. Then, one night, I had me some trouble with a limey sailor. He got mad at me 'cause he figgered I'd cheated him. Held out some of

the change he had comin'. Knocked me down, he did! Punched
me around 'til I got hold of a scantling 'bout six foot long and
busted his head.

"Nacherly, I was scared, and I run off. Lucky for me, an
old steamboat was jest pullin' out, and I jumped on board of
the barge they was towin'. The barge was loaded with hosses
they was takin' to Matagorda, Texas, and them hosses had
plenty of ginger in 'em. I had to jump around some jest to
keep outta their way. Leastways, at first I did. You see, I'd
never been 'round hosses much, but I liked 'em right off, and
they taken to me. By the time we got to Matagorda, they was
prac'ly eatin' outta my hand.

"The ranch foreman met us at the dock and seen how I was
makin' out with them critters, and he hired me on as a wrangler
for the drive to Atascosa; that's where the ranch was. Before
long, I was a full-fledged cowboy, and I been workin' at it
ever since . . ." His voice trailed off, and he glanced over towards me, his face flushing under the heavy tan.

"Well, will you listen to me! Runnin' off at the mouth like
some old back-yard biddy. Ain't like me to jabber away like
thet." He shook his head. "And you ain't wearin' no backwards
collar, neither."

I laughed. "Don't mind one little bit, Red, but I sure would
like to ask you a question."

"Yeah?" he replied. "What was you wantin' to find out?"

"Not much, really," I told him. "But I am sorta curious.
Did you hold out on that limey sailor's change?"

He was grinning broadly. "Course I did! Them fellers was
tighter'n the bark on a tree! I was lucky if I'd git a nickle for
doin' all thet runnin' around. Sometimes three cents was all
they'd hand over. Hell, I had to eat!"

The sun was down now, and it was getting very dark. The
river had left plenty of downed trees along the bank, and I was
finding it hard to show a path around them. Ahead, some fifty
yards or so, I could barely make out a small grove of cottonwoods, and I pointed them out to Garth.

"I'm thinkin' we'd best hole up right there," I told the
redhead. "Let's you'n me check it out."

We gigged the horses into a lope and headed that way. I
slipped the Henry out and held it at the ready. I watched the
chestnut's ears as we drew near, and he showed no signs of
alarm. There was a ring of rocks in the center of those trees,
so somebody had camped here at some time or another.

PLATTE RIVER CROSSING

Climbing down, I walked around and taken a good look for
signs of recent use. By then, it was too dark to really see much
of anything. However, it did seem like a good, easy-to-defend
position, and right now that was most important.

Anybody coming at us from the south or west would be in
sight long before they came within pistol range. The eastern
side of the grove set up against a sheer bluff, towering some
three hundred feet above. About a hundred yards north of us,
the river taken a bend, and the heavy brush that grew along
the bank offered concealment. This would be our weakest point,
but a few men with rifles would be able to defend it easily.
Or at least keep the attacker's heads down.

Garth led the stage through the cottonwoods and into the
clearing, while I whistled in my flankers. There were four good-
sized trees down that would make fine barricades, so I recruited
Knott, Garth, and Tom Brooke to help me drag them to where
they would do the most good.

It'd been a while since I'd walked behind a team. Back
when we'd cleared our place in Texas, we'd used wild steers
like teams of oxen. Course, we didn't work in the dark like
I'd have to do now, and that'd made it some easier. Anyway,
I figgered to give it a try.

"I'll need your lead team," I told Ada. "And that doubletree,
also. Then we'll have to shorten up them reins somehow. Aw
heck! I'll just coil 'em, and that'll do the trick. No sense in
switchin' with the wheeler's lines."

We unharnessed the teams, and I taken the leaders over to
one of the big deadfalls, dragging the doubletree behind. I
waved the others out of the way and told Goodson to set the
picket line for both our saddle stock and the rest of those stage
horses as close to the coach as possible.

"Red!" I hollered. "You'n Bowie git your ropes dabbed on
the butt end of this tree and bring the tag ends over here. That's
right! Git 'em on good, now! Now bring me the ends. *Bueno*!
That's just fine, boys!"

We tied the ropes up short, on the doubletree, and I gave
a "hup" to the teams. "Hiddap, horses," I grunted. "C'mon,
boys, dig in," I crooned to them. Slowly, ponderously, that
big tree started to pivot, branches snapping off and flying in
all directions as it rolled slightly and almost came to a stop.

"Tom!" I cried out. "Break out that rope of yours. Come
bear a hand! Git a loop on that stub, stickin' up there."

With the added help of Brooke's horse, the tree moved into

place and formed a near-impenetrable barrier on the one side
of the clearing. Gosh only knows how many critters we done
outta a home during the next hour, but we sure managed to
get the job done. We had us a real fort!

Two of those trees had been there for some time, and one
old Billy coon gave us a real scolding as we tore up what'd
been his happy home. On another tree, a couple of possums'd
been dispossessed, and a flushed-out jackrabbit sure spooked
my team when he ran right under their noses. They pawed at
the sky some, but there wasn't much they could do with the
heavy tree tied on behind.

Meantime, Goodson had gotten a small fire started so Ada
could get our supper prepared. Chilton and the Kid kept an eye
out for any unwelcome visitors as they helped grain the horses.
We had more'n enough nose bags to go around.

It was purely a strange situation. Here we were, thick as
fleas, with the men who'd held up the stage, banding together
against a common enemy, the raiding Indians. And as for me,
I'd even shot two of them, and one of those two men I now
felt was my friend! I shook my head. If somebody'd told me
a story like this, I'd figger it as just another big windy. One
of those tall tales you hear around a campfire. But there was
no doubting the seriousness of our situation here. We really
needed each other!

The coffee had boiled, and Ada'd set it aside to settle. She
had some thick slices of bacon frying, and the aroma had my
juices flowing. We'd have to eat in shifts so that constant watch
could be kept around our perimeter. With Rousseau dead, there
were eight of us left, counting Ada. I knew that she'd insist
on taking a turn, so that meant four could be on guard, while
four others slept. Sunup would be about a quarter to six, but
we'd see first light around five. The watches would have to be
about three hours each.

One thing, for sure; wouldn't do for me and Ada to be out
on watch at the same time. Just too easy, for me at least, to
be distracted. We'd have to be alert if we wanted to be still
wearing our hair, come daylight.

I'd heard, or I'd read somewhere, that Injuns didn't like to
fight at night. That if they happened to get themselves killed
in the dark, then their spirits would have to wander aimlessly
forever.

Now that may just be true about some Injuns, but I knew
of two young Kiowa bucks who weren't one bit worried when

they crept into our horse corral one night and climbed all over me! We'd managed to kill 'em both, but they died trying, and I'm sure they wound up wherever good fighters go.

Then you take them Cherokees, the ones that fought at Pea Ridge, in Arkansas, during the late war. In the dark of the moon, they went out and got in back of the Union troops the night before the battle. Snuck through the enemy lines and flanked 'em, by gosh! There were twelve hundred of 'em, and they were under the command of a reb general, Albert Pike, a fine souldier, but they were led by Gen. Stand Watie, and you can bet he was a Cherokee. Could be they were afraid of being killed at night, but it sure didn't stop 'em!

I decided that Ada should be on the first guard so's she would be rested, come morning. Red Garth was the most qualified to lead that watch, and with him I assigned the Cherry Creek Kid and Sam Goodson.

"By the time you folks git something to eat, it'll be almost nine o'clock," I told him. "You wake us at midnight."

"But thet way you're gonna have amost twice the time on guard," he protested. "T'ain't fair, no way you look at it. What's wrong? You worryin' 'bout my laig and the Kid's bad hand? Hell! I been bee-stung badder'n this!"

I shook my head. "I want Ada to git all the rest that she can," I told him. "She's gonna be doin' more'n anybody, come daylight. Anyways... I doubt I'll be sleepin', so you be sure and wake me anytime if you figger somethin's up."

CHAPTER 13

WE'D LET OUR FIRE DIE DOWN TO JUST A FEW glowing embers so the coffee'd stay hot enough to warm those on guard. I'd been unable to doze off as yet even though I *was* tired and really needed the rest. Knowing the dangers that could lurk out there, I was naturally wary, and my eyes just refused to close. Shielding a match under the blanket, I glanced at my old hunting case watch that'd been passed down from Grandpaw McCowan. It was coming on to eleven o'clock, and so far I'd not heard any sounds of activity other than our own.

Right now that's what was bothering me. No sounds! The normal night noises had just flat quit! The cicadas, whose pulsating, droning buzz filled the night, were stilled: then the cry of a questing nighthawk had choked off in midsound. Someone or something was out there prowling around!

Sitting up in my blanket, I slipped into my boots, rising to stand in the shadow of a cottonwood as I slung the holstered Remington around my waist. My hat, I left at the head of my bedroll so's to serve two purposes. One, because I figgered it would be a dead giveaway on my head, the other reason being to create the illusion of a man sleeping. When I'd rolled up, I'd taken off my spurs, so I had no reason to worry about them now. Slipping the thong off the hammer of my six-gun, I started towards Garth and Ada, who were slightly silhouetted on the far side of the clearing.

Keeping to the trees that bordered the edges, I got right up close before Garth was aware of my presence. "Quiet," I warned them. "I b'lieve we've got us some company, and they ain't makin' a social call. More'n likely they'll try runnin' off our horses, so I'm gonna head over that way. Stand by, now, you hear me! Make sure of your targets before you start blastin' away, but don't be afraid to shoot." I meant that mostly for Ada but didn't want to hurt her feelings by singling her out.

113

They both nodded, and I moved away silently. Goodson, a conscientious man, I'd stationed by the stage and the nearby picket line, while the Kid was hunkered down somewheres covering the bend of the river. Moving cautiously, I made a beeline for that side, using the trees for cover. I figgered I'd better let him know I was on the move, or he might be cutting loose on me.

As it was, I almost stumbled over him before he heard me coming. The sound of his hammer cocking was enough. Real quick like, I let him know who I was, and he lowered the gun.

"Wouldn't hurt none if you was to let a man know you was prowlin' around," he told me. "Why, I coulda shot you easy enough, and you'd be starin' up at them stars right now and not seein' nothin'!" His tone was reproachful as he turned the cylinder on around and let the hammer down on an empty.

"Somethin's wrong out there," he continued. "All at once them crickets quit chirpin', and I ain't heard a sound ever since. What do you make of it, McCowan?"

"It ain't no bear, nor no other critter," I told him. "We still got a fire goin', and they'd stay plumb away from that smell of smoke. No! I b'lieve we got us some Injuns hidin' there, and they'll mebbe try for the horses. You hang tight here and keep your eyes and ears open. I'm gonna take me a little *pasear* over to the stage and make sure they're awake there. Watch your topknot, Kid. Long time 'til daylight."

A shadowy form rose up directly in front of me. "What was you sayin' about daylight?" It was Bowie Knott, his hat already on his head and a gun in his hand.

"Yes! I heard that, too. What's up, Rush?" Ben Chilton was on his feet, also, and held his rifle at the ready. "The two of us decided to sleep over here," he explained. "Seemed the best thing to do, since this end is our weakest point to defend. What time is it, anyway?"

"It's only eleven or so," I told him. "But we might just have us some Injuns out there in the trees. Where's Brooke sleepin'? Is he here with you fellers?"

"Naw," replied the Kid. "He's rolled up under the stage. You want me to come along with you? You just might be needful of some help. No tellin' how many of them're out there. Could be there's more'n one man can handle."

"Thanks, Kid, but I need you right here for now. You're one-handed, anyway, and this might turn into a wrasslin' and skull-crackin' job. I will take Ben along, though. He's as big as a bear and probably twice as mean. C'mon, cap'n, we got us some scoutin' to do!"

For a big man, Ben moved along very quietly. I'd warned, or rather cautioned, him about making a lot of noise, but it wasn't at all necessary. He did reach out and take ahold of my belt so's to not lose each other in the dark.

Suddenly, a horse grunted and then whickered real loud and mad-sounding. There was a flurry of movement along that picket line, and several more of our horses joined in, whistling and stamping and jerking at the taut line.

A streak of flame lanced out from under the stage, coupled with a resounding boom, and a man screamed! Tearing from Chilton's grasp, I ran towards the shadowy figures outlined by the muzzle flash.

Dodging the hoofs of a rearing horse, I grappled with one of the intruders, back-heeling him to the ground. I'd caught a glimpse of moonlight glinting off his knife blade and made a grab for that wrist as we went down; rolling him over, my legs scissored around his waist.

Desperately, I slammed at his head with the heavy six-gun, while he struck at my face with his free fist and his teeth snapped dangerously close to my exposed throat. Another try closed on my shirt collar, and it ripped loose; his eyes all bulged out, and his face contorted with hate as we struggled. I tried to butt him in the face; then his knuckled fist caught me on the bridge of my nose, and the tears started.

I got the gun up under his chin, but he grabbed my wrist and pushed the revolver away before I could cock the hammer back. By now, it was sort of a Mexican standoff, with both of us straining to use our weapons with one hand and having to ward off our opponent's with the other.

As we rolled and thrashed around, I began to tighten that scissor hold on his waist, and slowly and inexorably, those legs, heavily muscled by years on horseback, began squeezing his life away. He tensed his belly, but it was too late. A last gasp and blood gushed from his open mouth; his grip on my wrist relaxed, and he was dead!

Vaguely, I'd been aware of gunshots and lots of yelling but had been too busy fighting for my life to be concerned. Now, staggering to my feet, I swayed unsteadily and looked around. A hand came down on my shoulder, and I twisted violently around, jamming my cocked gun into somebody's belly!

"Hold off, Rush! It's me!" Ben Chilton, his face blood-

streaked, was holding up a hand as if to ward me off. "The
fight's over, Rush! Those we didn't kill have all run away.
We're safe now, at least for a while. Are you hurt?"

"I'm all right," I told him. "How'd we make out? Did we
lose anybody? Where's Ada? Is she okay?"

"I guess so," he replied. Then, looking around, he said,
"I . . . I don't know, Rush. I haven't seen her. My God! We
better start looking for her. If she's hurt or killed . . ."

My heart started pounding, and I grabbed him by the shirt
front, jerking him forward. "Start looking, damn you! Help
me find her! She's gotta be somewheres!"

Brooke materialized out of the darkness. "Ada is fine, Rush,
but I'm afraid Goodson is dead. I was asleep when it happened,
but his thrashing around awakened me.

"He was leaning against the coach," he went on. "I spoke
to him just before I dozed off. Asked him to call me a bit early
so I'd have time to take care of personal things before I went
on guard.

"They apparently got in close before he was aware of it,
and one of them cut his throat. He fell right next to where I
was lying and jerked around rather violently. Kicked me, as a
matter of fact, and that's what woke me up. I was able to kill
one of them with my short rifle." He looked down. "I've no
excuse for what happened next. I'm rather shamed.

"I'm afraid I lost my wits for a moment. Completely, it
seems. Forgot to reload the weapon and then used it like a
club. Lashed about, don't you know, and managed to kill one
more of the buggers. I really don't know what came over me!
Not something that one of good breeding, like myself, should
ever allow. I'm aware now that being civilized is a rather thin
veneer. You must excuse me. I'd like to wash myself."

Chilton and I both stared after him. He'd spoken with obvious sincerity, there was no doubt of that. Brooke was a good
man. One worth riding the river with!

Red Garth limped over and joined us. "I don't know how,
but we sure enough scared 'em off," he said. "Would you
believe, Rush, that girl shot one of 'em! Saved my bacon, she
did! There was two of them red devils jumped me 'n her, both
of 'em comin' in on us at the same time."

"What happened," I asked him. "You mean, *she* had to kill
one of 'em? What were *you* doin' while Ada was shootin' the
Injun? I put her over with you so's she'd be safe!"

Busy reloading his cap-and-ball Colt, he taken a moment

before answering. "Well, sir," he told us, "no more'n a minute or so after we heard a gun go off near the stage, there they were! Two of 'em, and both had guns! I plugged one of 'em, and he fell ag'in me, wrappin' me up with his arms. It was touch and go, I want to tell you! There I was, fightin' this feller who didn't have sense enough to know he was already dead . . . He tripped me, and down we went, with him all twined around me so's I couldn't get my gun into play.

"Out of the corner of one eye, I see the other Injun comin' for me and seem's like he's wantin' to dance, too. Has an old sawed-off musket up to his shoulder, and he's tryin' his durndest to git a clear shot at me. I don't reckon he'd even seen Ada, and me'n the first Injun are rollin' around."

"Yeah?" we chorused. "What happened then?" I asked.

"Why, thet li'l gal jest blew thet Injun plumb outta his moccasins! Got him with the right-hand barrel of thet scatter gun. Put a hole in him you could drive a wagon through! If there was any more of them Injuns out there waitin' so's they could help, she sure put the fear of God into 'em!

"Me, I finally got my six-gun up into the armpit of Mister Injun, the one who was too durn stubborn to die. This time, he was dead for sure! Scattered pieces of him over half the trees on that end of the clearing. Tell you one thing. We make a good team, thet gal and me! She can ride along with me any day of the week and twice on Sundays!"

"How's she takin' it?" I asked him. "Killin' a man's not easy for anybody, much less a nice girl like Ada."

"Not too good," he replied. "Wouldn't hurt was you to go on over there and comfort her some. She was cryin' . . ."

"What will we do about Goodson," asked Chilton. "At this rate, that stage'll be full of bodies. Shall we bury him?"

Another friend dead. I'd almost forgotten the price we had paid for our small victory. "Not a chance," I told him. "Sam Goodson earned his place on that stage!" It was then I noticed the blood on his face and could see it was fresh.

"Look's like you've been hurt, Ben," I told him. "You've blood all over your face, and it's still drippin'."

"I do?" His expression was ludicrous. Touching a hand up to his head, he felt around and winced. "Ouch! You sure are right! I've been wounded and didn't even know it! Now that's something, isn't it? I don't even remember."

"Let's move on over by the fire, and we'll take a look at it, Ben. By the way, where's your cap?"

He shook his head in wonderment. "Beats me! Might've come off during the scuffle. It's around here someplace."

As we moved off towards the fire, Ben did a little dance and whistled a tune. He seemed to be in good spirits, and I asked him why.

"Why? Why, because we fought 'em off, that's why! Ain't nothing going to stop us from going on to the fort now. We have all those Indians on the run, Rush!"

"You couldn't be more wrong," I told him. "The Injuns we fought tonight were just a few young bloods tryin' to git some horses and count coup on us. The main bunch is yet to come. They'll hold off until just before sunrise. Then we *will* see some Injuns! Hundreds of Injuns! Save them words until we've driven through the gates of the fort. Listen to me, Ben. The real fight's still to come, and we'll be lucky as hell if any of us make it to Fort Kearny and the Platte River crossing! About all we can do is to make them really pay a high price for us. Kill as many of 'em as we can."

He nodded soberly. "I guess I didn't realize or just didn't think hard about our situation. If what that messenger said is true, they'll have us outnumbered forty to one. Those are pretty overwhelming odds, aren't they? Well, like you said, all we can do is to kill as many as we can. Raise the cost so high they'll hesitate to attack another stage."

In the flickering firelight, we found a deep cut in Ben's scalp. Looked like a glancing wound from a bullet, deep enough to lay a finger in it. I started to explain the difficulties of bandaging a wound like that, and he understood. It would require cutting a lot of his hair off, and it would heal all right without that. We rubbed in some lard so it was more or less covered. Ben didn't complain.

I found Ada at the far side of the clearing, sitting down on one of the deadfalls, her face in her hands. As I neared her, she raised her head and wiped at her face.

"H'lo, Rush," she said quietly. "Guess you think I'm an old crybaby, huh? Well . . . I can't help it, honest. I just never dreamed that I'd ever have to *kill* somebody. I know, and I agree that it had to be done, but it doesn't make the actual killing any easier to forget." Her head lowered, and her shoulders began to shake.

"Look," I told her. "Supposing . . . just supposing Garth had been killed by that Injun. How would you feel then?"

Before she could answer, I went on. "If he killed Red Garth, then he'd've made a try at killin' you. Would you be reluctant then? Would you just stand there and let him do whatever he wanted?" My voice had grown in volume as I let my anxiety turn to anger.

Then, quietly, I continued. "Course you wouldn't, Ada. You'd have shot him down like he deserved, and you'd have a good reason to quiet your poor conscience. Red Garth dead! He killed Red Garth, so you killed him! Now! How is there, or *is* there, any difference?

"You did the right thing, Ada," I told her. "You killed a man because he was trying to kill your friend. You saved a friend's life, Ada, and you should be proud of it! So! You git on back to the stage and try to git some rest. Lots of work for you tomorrow. You gotta drive that stage!"

She nodded but didn't look at me. I watched as she got to her feet and walked slowly towards the stage. I hoped that what I'd said would help, but I couldn't be sure. Only time would tell, and we didn't have a whole lot of that.

CHAPTER 14

⟨⟨

THAT COFFEE WAS PRETTY STRONG! IT'D BEEN ON the fire for at least six hours, half boiling most of the time. When I poured myself a cup, I commented on the color.

"Look's more like river mud than anything else," I said. "Chances are, if I was to dip me some water outta the Little Blue and warm it in this pot, nobody'd know the difference. Just goes to show you. You git folks to thinkin' one way, and they just take it for granted no matter what."

"Wait a minute." As I stared down into that cup, something, an idea, came into my mind! Excitedly, I called over to the others to gather 'round.

"I just got me an idea," I told them. "Now we've decided that our best chance lies in stayin' here in these trees where we've got good cover against an attack. Right? We'll mebbe still git killed, but we'll take a lot of them Injuns right along with us. We know it, and they know it, too."

Most everybody nodded or spoke out in agreement. "Well," I said, "that's right! It is the best way, and anybody will tell you just that! Out in the open, them Injuns would sure wipe us out in no time a-tall."

I could see some puzzled expressions on the faces of most of them; leastways, the ones nearest to the firelight. Then Ben Chilton figgered it was time that *he* said something.

"We couldn't agree with you more, Rush, but what on earth are you jabbering about? Of course it's safer here! That's why we picked this place to fort up." He turned to the rest of them, hunching his shoulders, his arms outspread. "Can you quit talking in circles and tell us your idea?" he asked. "We aren't, none of us, mind readers, you know."

I tossed out the coffee and set the cup down. "Okay," I told them. "Here is my plan. Some time back we passed a creek drainin' into the river. Like I told Ada, that there stream had

120

to be Thirty-two-Mile Creek and meant we had no more'n a thirty-five mile run to Fort Kearny. Now we've come quite some distance since we passed that creek, so that means not only are we closer to the fort, but we're also way above any of them stations that were burned out." I paused. "Well, I'm sorry, folks. I just gotta roll me a smoke!"

Despite the groans and smart remarks, I didn't resume my little discussion until I had that cigarette fired up. A couple of big puffs and I was all set.

"All right! I believe we could drive right on outta here tonight if we play it right! Like I said, them Injuns have already made up their minds that we're gonna stay here and make our fight. Once they figgered that out, they must have made some plans of their own. They *know* we'd be real dumb if we left the safety of this here grove of trees. Watched as we drug them dead trees around to make us a barricade."

I held up my hand as several tried to talk all at once. "Wait, now. Give me a chance to speak my piece. Now there ain't no doubt in my mind that it'd be easier if we was to leave the stage behind. But that would mean all of them friends of ours would have to stay behind. I'd speaking of the poor dead ones in that stage.

"Now I been called a stubborn man, and mebbe that is the gospel truth, because I ain't gonna see them left behind so them Injuns can cut 'em up and have their way with 'em. We McCowans have some mighty set rules we live by, and not one of us has ever abandoned a friend dead or alive.

"Besides—" this I said with a grin on my face—"I'd be willin' to bet hard money that all of you folks would be mighty proud if we could come drivin' through that gate in that there coach just as if them Injuns didn't mean no more to us than a bad rainstorm! Am I right?"

It started as a murmur, but it grew right into a roar. A mighty big roar of approval. "You durn betcha," cried Red.

"Sound's good to me," hollered the Kid.

It was plain to see they all approved of my plan. Now all we had to do was do it! Quickly, I outlined the particulars and assigned those who were best suited to what had to be done.

"I don't believe that river is too deep to wade," I said. "But I better have a coupla good swimmers just in case. We are gonna go out that way. Ben! Being a sea captain, you'd have to be a first-class swimmer, so you're one." As I said this, I noticed he was shaking his head and waggling a hand at me, so I asked what he wanted.

"I can't swim a stroke, Rush. Never learned, and I never wanted to. You see, when you're way out there on that huge ocean, being able to swim would only prolong the agony. Say your ship sinks, for instance, and you're hundreds of miles away from the shore. What good would it do you if you were able to swim? Better to drown right off and not have that suffering to go through. Nope! I can't swim!"

Brooke and Bowie Knott volunteered. I walked down near the water with them and told them what I needed to know. "Mainly, I want you to scout it out and make sure no Injuns are over on the other side. I don't b'lieve they are 'cause I ain't seen no movement over there, but you never know. It would be the last way they'd figger us to follow, 'cause that is where all them attacks have taken place. Find me a shallow ford where we can take the stage across. Then go further in and make sure we ain't gonna bog down before we've got clear of this place and clean outta sight. Don't go in too far, 'cause we ain't got all the time in the world. I'll expect you back in no more'n half an hour."

Both stripped down to their underwear, and I cautioned my Texan friend Bowie to take along his boots. Brooke already had his hung around his neck by a thong. "You'll need them boots," I told him, "when you git over in them rocks on the far side. 'Sides, I been seein' lots of sand burrs layin' around, and they can be hell on bare feet. You'all git goin' now, and don't be stayin' away too long, y'hear?"

Bowie taken along his navy Colt, and I watched as Brooke set his four-barreled derringer on his head and tugged that funny-looking cap down over it. They waded out a ways, then ducked down to where the water was up to their necks. In a moment, they were out of my sight.

Returning to the fire, I sent the Kid out to scout. "Be darn sure you keep outta sight," I told him. "All I need to know right now is how them Injuns is spread out. Don't go beyond the edge of the grove, and don't take no potshots at any Injuns you see no matter how temptin' it looks. Okay?"

His eyes were shining bright as diamonds, and it was easy to see he enjoyed the prospect. "Count on me, Rush. Plenty of time to *shoot* Injuns. Right now I'm gonna outfox 'em!"

Ben had finished greasing the wheel hubs like I'd asked and was hanging the bucket back where it belonged. He stood there, staring at his hands and forearms, which were liberally smeared with the black, tarry substance. Reaching up, he started to scratch his head, but caught himself in time.

"Try usin' some of that sand along the river bank," I told him. "That'll take off the worst of it; then you can finish with some soap. I'm curious, Ben. Why wasn't you usin' the brush that was in the bucket? Seem's like that'd been some easier, and you wouldn't have got yourself all greasy."

He smiled ruefully. "Didn't notice it until I'd gotten a handful," he said. "By then, it was too late. What'd you want me to do next?"

"Just be ready to pull out," I told him. "By that I mean gather up your duds and make sure they're on the stage. Me and you and Tom Brooke will be the rear guard. It'll be up to us to convince them Injuns that we're all of us still in this here grove. We'll have to run around a bit and act as if there's seven of us in here instead of just three. Make them think we're gittin' set to hold 'em off, come daylight. We gotta keep that up 'til the stage is well away and then ride like hell to catch up. Can you handle that, Ben?"

He nodded soberly, and I went on. "The key to my plan is to have fresh horses waitin' further up the line. We've got enough stock to do that, and there lies our advantage."

"How do you plan to arrange that?" he asked me. "We only have six of us left that can ride and handle a gun. If the three of us are held up here in the grove, how will we move those extra horses? The Kid has a bad hand."

"Okay," I told him, "here's what we do. Red Garth and Bowie Knott are the handiest at handlin' a rope. That stage will need help crossin' the river, what with all the weight and the muddy bottom. Ada'll be drivin', naturally, and the Kid'll ride up on the box with her in case they'd run into any trouble. He'll have them two .44 Remingtons, and we'll put one of the shotguns up there for extra protection.

"Soon as Brooke and Bowie git back, I'm gonna git them to haze all the extra stock across the river and out on picket a mile or so further in. We can help them with the crossing part, but we'll break off and come back here.

"Next comes the stage. Garth and Knott will git ropes on each side and help the stage make the crossing. You, me, and Brooke will start our shenanigans about then. Build up the fire, make some noise, and let on like we're addin' some stuff to the barricades.

"Once the stage is across the river and on solid ground, Garth and Knott will go on ahead, pick up the horses, and be on their way. I figger, roughly, that we'll be about thirty miles from the fort when we hit the main stage road. So it will be up to Garth and Knott to drive them horses, say, halfway up that road. Then they'll just set and wait for us to come along. Wherever they hold up, that will be our relay point, and we'll switch teams and saddle stock right there. We'll have to be quick about it, because I figger by then a few of them Injuns are gonna be right on our tails."

"How long will we have to keep up our pretense?" he asked me. "What if they find out before the stage has time to get clear? We have to give them credit for a little sense. The Indians may be watching us right now. They may have scouts out there in the trees, following our every move."

"That's why I sent the Kid out there," I told him. "He's makin' sure that they ain't in close like that. 'Sides, my whole scheme is built on them thinkin' the obvious. Like we talked about a while back. It don't make hardly any sense for us to leave an easily defended position and risk everything by runnin' away. I'm countin' on them Injuns thinkin' *we've* got better sense. Let's hope I'm right!"

"Yeah!" he agreed. Then, thoughtfully, he said, "You know, now that I think about it, I've always been sort of a fatalistic person. What will be, will be, if you know what I mean. I had many narrow escapes in my years at sea and also on the land. Matter of fact—" he chuckled—"some of the closest calls have been on the waterfront, in countries all over the world. Plenty of rats around the pier, and lots of them walking on two legs.

"I've had to more or less accept things. Go along with a situation rather than fight it. Sometimes I feel like our futures are all written down somewhere. Even the time we'd die has already been decided. Maybe written down in a book and kept up to date by some old man, sporting a long white beard and wearing a nightgown. Don't look at me like maybe I'm crazy! I'm not the only man who feels this way. It seems to be common among men who take chances. I'm sort of surprised that you haven't gotten around to feeling more or less the same way. You've apparently put your life on the line more than once."

He was right, of course, and I told him so. "But I feel that every now and then we come to a sort of crossroad and what happens after that depends on which fork we choose. I reckon we've about talked ourselves out, Ben. You better be gittin'

that grease off your hands, and quick like. Tom and Bowie
Knott should be showin' up here soon, and we'll be all ready
to pull out." Ben nodded and left for the river.

Ada had taken the time to make fresh coffee, and I accepted
a cup gratefully. Together we sat down by the fire, a moment
of thoughtful silence following.

"What do you honestly think of our chances?" Ada asked.
"I know you've seemed very optimistic, but I wondered if you
were just trying to cheer us up. Even now I feel like there's
no escape. That we've no way to avoid a fight and certainly
no way to win. I'm sorry, Rush, dear. I just can't help feeling
the way I do. Like there's no help and we'll all be dead tomorrow. Or worse," she added, her face bleak. Then, squaring
her shoulders, she looked up at me, a tender expression sof-
tening her features. "If anyone could pull this off, Rush, I
know it would be you. Forgive me for being so gloomy. It'll
pass, and I'll be just fine!"

I reached out and taken her hand. "Don't start worryin' your
pretty little head about gittin' killed, boss. We got us a stage
run to finish and some passengers to take in to Fort Kearny.
Worry about keepin' a schedule, not about a bunch of Injuns
that don't amount to a hill of beans. We're gonna make it just
fine! You trust in your old Uncle Rush."

I stood up as Bowie and Tom Brooke showed at the edge
of the firelight. They were back in their clothes and had big
grins on their faces. Matter of fact, Tom was beaming!

"We got her made, Rush," said Bowie. "There'll be no real
problem crossin' that li'l old river," he continued. "Found a
shallow fordin' place mebbe fifty paces upstream, and it has
good solid bottom with no signs of quicksand."

"Yes! And we found no trace of any redskins," added Tom.
"From up on the hillside, we could see a great many cooking
fires and several hundred Indians, but they're more or less
concentrated on the north and the south sides. I would imagine
that since they've literally *stripped* the countryside to the west,
they'll never expect us to try that direction."

"What I'm hopin' is that they won't expect us to try *any*
direction. We want them to think we're trapped in here and
will stay and fight to the last man. Or woman," I added.

"You boys did just fine," I told them. "Now! Let's throw
the harness on them stage teams and git ready to roll out!"

Garth had been busy rigging halter leads on all our spare
horses. There were fourteen head to take to where we planned

to make the relay change. Since there would be five men on horseback and we'd need six fresh horses for the stage, this meant we had three extra mounts. I made a quick decision and acted on it right away!

"I want three of them horses left for us," I told Red. "I got a hunch we just might be needin' some spares. When our decoy job is all done here, you folks will have gotten about an hour's start. That is, if we can fool 'em for that long a time. Chances are we'll be about one step ahead of a lot of *mad* Injuns, and we'll need all the help we can git. The spare mounts might just make the difference!" I turned back to Garth and stuck a big, wide smile on my face.

"Leave me that chestnut of yours for a spare, Red. Any of the other horses will do me fine for the first half-hour ride so long as he's got four legs and a place to strap on my saddle. How about it, Red, old friend?"

Garth just grinned and handed me the halter rope. I was naturally very appreciative of his kindness, and I told him so. "Don't you worry none," I said. "I won't run him harder than I have to, and I'll make sure you git him back."

"You'd better take good care of him," he told me, "'cause he's your horse from now on. I just give him to you!"

Well, sir! I didn't know *what* to say, so I just didn't say a durn thing! This was a mighty fine horse and wasn't just an ordinary gift. I'd met fellers who'd kill for a horse like this! Garth had told me square out that he owned the horse and had a bill of sale for him. Seem's his old boss back there in Texas had given him the chestnut. Garth saved the feller's life one day when he'd got hung up on some fool bronc with his spur caught in the cinch ring. Red had run the horse down and extricated his boss, durn near ruinin' himself in the process. I'd find a way to square up, I promised myself that, and we'd both be the richer for it.

Ada and the Cherry Creek Kid were about ready to leave. Seemed strange calling Halloran the "Kid." He'd admitted to being over thirty, and his gray hair made him look a lot more'n that. Another good man, I thought to myself, and he more than pulled his weight despite the injured hand.

Red Garth had led out the spare string, with Bowie by his side. We'd have to give them time to tie them horses on the other side and cross again to help with the coach. But we could move the stage down close to the river. I rode my new horse up close to the box and spoke with Ada. This was our good-by, really. I wouldn't see her again until we reached the relay point. Right now was the time for us to start in doing our shenanigans. The diversion that the others would need to slip away.

"You take care of yourself, Rush," she told me. "Don't be trying to play the hero. Just do what has to be done, use a little common sense, and don't let yourself be hurt. Take care, Rush. Of yourself and the others. I care for you. I really do! I sure don't want to lose you, my dear." A tear showed in each eye as she turned away, and I felt a lump in my throat as big as an apple.

CHAPTER 15

XXXXXXXXXXXXXXXXXXXXXXXXXXXXXXXXXXXXXXXXXXXXXXXXXXXXX

I HAD SURE ENOUGH CALLED THE TURN WHEN I'D predicted being only one step ahead of some mighty mad Injuns. We were not much more'n that right now, and my horse was staggering on his last legs. Looking back, I could see what must be at least half the Sioux nation hot on our heels. It was about time for us to switch mounts! If we could do it without us getting killed in the process, we'd be mighty lucky!

We'd been fairly successful in fooling them, at least for the first half hour or so. Built up the one fire and even lit another smaller one. Rode around dragging more trees and piling them against the barricades. Seemed like we were going to fool them completely.

I'd decided to put my saddle on the chestnut and ride my first horse bareback. Rigged a rope bridle and ran a short length of rope around his middle to tuck my knees under. I figgered I could just slip off him when the time came so's I wouldn't lose any time. It was a good idea, and the other boys had done the same. It looked like my idea might be the extra inch that would save us being caught. As tired as my horse might be, he couldn't be any more so than those Injun ponies so close behind us.

I swore silently to myself. If I hadn't been so all-fired cocky about fooling them Injuns, we might have slipped away without a soul knowing we'd gone. Seemed like it sure was going good! That old fire was just a-blazing away, with me and the others trotting around the clearing and piling up more logs, so I decided to sing!

I started out with one of my favorites, old "Dixie," and as any patriotic southern boy would do, I sang it sorta loud. Naturally, Tom Brooke joined right in, and after a minute or so, Ben Chilton decided it was his turn. Being a Yankee, he started bellering "The Battle Hymn of the Republic." Them two songs just don't seem to go well together.

Me'n Tom was singing "Advance the flag of Dixie! Hurrah! Hurrah!" when Ben comes back with "Let the hero, born of woman, crush the serpent with his heel," and the fight was on.

I hauled that chestnut's head around and charged on into Ben's sorrel. As we came together, I sorta come off of that chestnut and brought Ben to the ground. Next thing I knowed, we commenced swinging at each other, and Ben fetched one up alongside my head that made my ears ring!

Tom Brooke had got down off his horse and was trying his durndest to break us apart when he seen two Injuns sneaking into the clearing. Reckon they was wondering what tricks we were up to and had come on over to investigate.

Tom's rifle was hanging on his saddle horn, but he grabbed that little four-barreled pepperbox and started firing. I seen the one Injun go down, and the other clutched at one of his legs. Then the little gun was empty, and we had to just lay there and watch that wounded Injun limp outta sight.

I reckon it was pure-D luck, but Tom's first slug hit the one Injun right smack in his eye, and he was dead before he hit the ground. The other one had gotten away, and you sure could bet hard money he'd be back, and not by his lonesome.

We didn't waste any time hanging around; you could bet a hundred dollars on that. The fires would burn out, so there was no reason to bother with them. Real quick like, I caught up my spare horse and swung onto his back. Tom was already mounted, but Ben was having trouble with his horse. Scared, the horse kept backing away and throwing his head up. Ben, in frustration, was jerking on the rope bridle, scaring that poor critter even more. Finally, I was able to grab hold of the bridle, and Ben threw himself up on the horse's back.

"Sorry I smacked you in the head," he shouted. "Hope you won't hold a grudge!"

"Nah!" I hollered back. "I'm sorry I stuck my old thumb in your eye. Can you see all right? We'd better be burnin' tracks up the trail. Them Injuns sure won't be far behind!"

And, like I just said, they *were* real close! We would have to make the switch in mounts without any chance of error, or we'd be dead! Them Injuns would swarm all over us!

"About that time!" I hollered out real loud as I pulled the chestnut in close. "You boys take care now, y'hear! We got 'em licked if we can make this switch! We'll leave 'em behind like they was standin' still!"

It went slicker'n grease for me. Turning sideways, with the chestnut running smoothly alongside, I just stuck a foot in the stirrup and heaved myself across. One quick glance at my two companions and I socked the spurs home, leaving a badly tired horse far behind. A coupla hundred yards further on, I looked back and was relieved to find both Tom and Ben close behind me. The Injuns were dropping back.

I pulled the chestnut down to a ground-eating lope, and a moment later, my friends caught up. "Well!" I hollered. "I had my doubts for a little while, but we beat 'em. Them old Injun ponies'll never catch us now!"

Ben had a pained expression, and I saw he wasn't sitting, least not solidly, in his saddle. More like standing in his stirrups. He caught my look and grimaced. "Believe I'll stick to ships," he said. "Lot easier on a man's anatomy."

"Well," I replied, "we can take it easier on these horses now. Them Injuns have turned back. I don't reckon we'll be bothered by that bunch anymore. If we hold these horses at a good steady lope, we'll catch up with the others soon."

"I'm sure glad to hear that," said Ben. "If I never ride another horse, it'll be too soon. Bad enough with a saddle, but riding bareback is pure torture! That nag I was riding had a backbone like a bucksaw blade. When we do catch up, I plan to ride in the stage for the rest of the way."

Tom and I exchanged amused glances. "It's really not a difficult accomplishment," said Tom. "Just a matter of getting toughened up. In certain areas of the body," he added. "Now, me! I become violently ill every time I even *see* a ship! Crossing the Atlantic was sheer agony for me. No matter how many times I try, I still become seasick."

"Never been on a ship," I told them. "But I reckon I must have been born on a horse." I leaned towards Ben. "Tom's right," I told him. "It's just a matter of gittin' accustomed to it. Cheer up! We ain't got too far to go now!"

About two hours later, we topped out on a little rise to find the coach less than a half mile ahead. Our horses were still full of ginger and hadn't even worked up a sweat. My chestnut's ears flipped forward when he spotted those ahead of us, and he wanted to run! Twisted his head back and was sort of running sideways, picking his feet high.

"Take it easy, old son," I told him. "We got all the fun ahead of us now. We can take all the time in the world!"

Ada must have slowed the stage because we caught up real soon. Both she and the Kid had big grins, and he seemed to be real glad to see us. Don't get me wrong! Ada was, too; I could see that, but I expected it from her. After all, we'd said things to each other. I'd never kissed the Kid!

They were both trying to ask us questions, but what with all the racket the horses made and the harness jingling, it was nigh to impossible to make ourselves heard.

"Wait 'til we git to the relay point," I hollered. "Then we'll tell you the whole story!" The stage horses were some lathered up, and I'd no doubt they could use some rest. Not too bad, though, considering how far they'd come and all of that weight they were pulling. One thing—the road was a lot smoother than that one we'd followed along the river.

Some distance ahead, I could see a darker patch near the side of the road. It didn't have enough height to be trees, so it could well be our relief horse herd. Seemed to me it was moving around a bit, like a horse cavvy might do, but my eyes could be playing tricks on me at that distance.

Another quarter mile, and now I could tell for sure that it was horses. Reckon I was still a little spooked by all I seen in the past three days because an ugly thought popped into my mind! Sure! It was horses, all right, but were our friends up there with them? Could just as well be Injuns.

"I'm gonna ride up a ways," I told Tom, "just to be sure that everything's all right. Chances are I'll have to wake them fellers up so's they can have the teams ready. I want you'n Ben to stick close to Ada. Anything happens up there ahead, you turn and run and make sure she runs with you! I won't be able to do much if it is Injuns up there, but the devils'll know they been in a fight!"

He squinted at me from under the bill of that funny cap he was wearing. "Do you think there may be Indians ahead? This whole area has been burned out. Why would you expect a group of Indians around here?"

"I don't!" I told him. "But it's better to be safe than sorry. Leastwise, that's what my old grandmaw used to say."

The chestnut was aching to run, and when I touched him in the flank, he really flattened out! Lucky for me I'd tied a hat cord under my chin, or I'd have lost the dern thing!

Halfway down the road, towards the horse herd, one of the

riders broke away and started in my direction. It was good old
Bowie Knott, by golly, and he'd jerked his hat off, waving it
around in the air! Faintly, I could hear what sounded pretty
much like our old rebel yell, and I yelled back.

"Heee haaaa!" I yelled at the top of my lungs as I came
thundering down on him, my chestnut really running proud.

"By gum Sally, you made it!" he hollered. He had his gun
in his right hand, like mebbe he'd been expecting trouble.

"Can't shake your hand less'n you put that hog leg away,"
I told him, sticking my hand out. He looked at the gun like he
wondered where it'd come from, then thrust it in the holster
and grinned at me.

"Damn!" he cried. "I'm sure enough glad to see you! How
did it go back there? Did you git away without them knowin'?
Must not have had any fuss with 'em. Thet horse ain't even
winded. Reckon you got plumb away!"

"Tell you all about it when we git where we're goin'," I
told him. "Let's git the stage teams changed and head on in to
Fort Kearny. I'm gittin' hungry, and I don't see a chuck wagon
nowheres around here."

The stage was coming up on us, so we turned towards where
the horses were being held and stayed at an easy lope. The
stage kept pace, and ever so often, Ada would glance over at
us and smile. She sure looked good up there!

Seemed like it only taken minutes to switch the teams. I
decided to stay with the chestnut because he was still just as
fresh as could be. Then we were on our way. The end of the
run was in sight!

The land we were passing over was rolling plain, with an
occasional clump of trees here and there. Good grazing for
cattle, and I was surprised not to see any signs of ranches.
Course the Injuns had been bothersome, but that never seemed
to stop the ranchers back in Texas. We'd had our share in the
Val Verde, what with the Kiowas and the Comanches going
down into Mexico to raid. Our place was right in the middle
of what they called the Comanche War Trail!

We'd been rolling for over an hour now, and I figgered a
stop for water would be a good idea. Up ahead was a grove,
and chances were we'd find a creek nearby. I pointed, making
the motions of drinking from a glass, and Ada nodded.

Chilton had meant what he said about riding in the stagecoach, and I suspected he was asleep right now. Red Garth
and I were alongside the coach, while Bowie and Tom Brooke

had some sort of discussion going behind us. I heard a word or two, and it was something about England.

We were drawing close to the trees now, and I saw a spot of blue just beyond. Some sort of pond, I figgered. Dense foliage covered the area surrounding the trees, and I guessed it might be berry vines. Ada turned off the road, steering the horses under the trees where there'd be some shade.

Suddenly, bright colors could be seen between the trees, and a rifle boomed! Injuns! Painted riders surged out from the grove and were all around us!

Ada screamed, and I saw her slump down in the box as the horses slammed into their collars and taken off in a panic. Garth was firing his Winchester, working that lever without taking the gun from his shoulder. I wheeled around to stay out of his line of fire and raked the chestnut's flanks.

Out on the road now, and I rammed the Henry's barrel into an Injun's gut, knocking him from his pony. A bullet tugged at my shirt, and a white-hot brand seared my hip. In behind me, I could hear screams of fear and anger and more shots.

More ponys were crowding me, and I smashed the butt of my Henry against a head that was looming over me. Reaching on around with my left hand, I got the Remington from my holster and triggered it into an Injun's face 'til he threw his hands up and disappeared under my horse's hoofs. More guns were going off, and the acrid bite of powder smoke filled my eyes. A rage was building in me. A berserk urge to kill!

The Henry's hammer fell on an empty chamber, and I started flailing at the bodies crowding in with the heavy barrel end, heedless of whether I struck friend or foe. The dense white powder smoke hung over us like a pall, and it was impossible to see clearly. Now the revolver was empty, and in my hate and anger, I smashed it onto a shaven head, watching the blood spurt as the skull shattered.

Then I was clear of the press of bodies and free of that cloud of gun smoke. Far down the road, I saw the stage, with Ada still aboard, careening down the rutted track. Spurring the chestnut savagely, I raced in pursuit!

Behind me, I heard more shots and the beat of hoofs. My horse shuddered as a bullet raked the pommel of the saddle and plowed into the fleshy part of his neck. A second round struck him on the rump, and he broke stride and almost went down. I brought his head back up and socked in the spurs.

God! Keep this horse on his feet, I prayed silently. One

final bullet sang past my ear, and the sound of hoofs to the rear was growing fainter. I risked a glimpse and watched a lone pursuer rein up and turn back.

The chestnut's breathing was sounding hoarse now, but we were gaining on the coach. "C'mon, boy," I whispered. "She isn't far off now." Leaning well forward on his withers, I got my weight off his kidneys and whispered more encouragement. "You can do it, boy! We're almost there now!"

A final burst of speed, and I was even with the wheelers. Slowly, we pulled ahead, and now the swing was alongside, in panic, his eyes opened wide and nostrils distended.

"Little bit more, boy. That's it! Little more and I'll have it! There!"

I'd grabbed the near leader's bridle by the cheek plate, and I set the chestnut down hard on his haunches, bringing the stage to a shuddering, harness-jingling halt!

Sliding to the ground, I ran back and leaped up into the box. Ada was lying in the boot, her face white and a wound seeping blood through the shoulder of her blouse. She moaned as I lifted her to the seat, and her eyes flickered open for a moment and then closed again. I propped up a valise and gently leaned her against it. I had to make sure the horse would be all right before we headed for the fort.

Loosening both cinches, I wiped some of the lather off of him and said what a fine horse he was and what a good job he had done. The wound in his neck was a shallow one, and I plastered it with grease from the stage's axle. That wound in his rump was deep, and the bullet was still in there. It would have to come out, of course, but it would heal. There would be a vet at the fort, I was sure, and he'd do the job for me. Leading him around to the rear of the stage, I took off the saddle and blanket and stowed them in the boot. I tied the reins to a stanchion and gave him a final pat.

The ride in to the fort was uneventful. A guard on duty at the gate pointed out the post hospital, and I drove over there. A surprised sentry ushered me in to the doctor, with Ada in my arms. They put her in a private room immediately and told me to go see the commandant.

"Will she be all right?" I asked the doctor. He was some older than me, but not much. I'd always thought of doctors as older men, and I wasn't sure I could trust this one.

"It's a serious wound, but she's very young and won't be

long in healing. Right now she needs plenty of rest and a few good meals." He patted me on the shoulder.

"Come back in the morning. She'll be more coherent then, and you may visit her. Incidentally, what is her name? We'll need that for our records." I told him, and he thanked me.

The same sentry told me where I'd find the commandant, so I figgered I'd best get it over with and headed that way.

Another sentry and another explanation, then I was allowed in. The commandant, a lieutenant colonel name of Crandall, was very friendly and very much interested in what I had to say to him. He waved me to a chair and poured us each a drink.

"We knew they were out for blood," he told me, "but never dreamed they would attack and burn the stations. I have only a token force here in the fort. We are here to protect and advise the emigrants heading west. If they have as big a force as you have described, they could easily overwhelm and even take over this post."

He drank from his glass and went on. "I'm afraid that this is more a matter for the civil authorities. Now that I know what they have done, I will notify Omaha. They'll take proper action and see that Miss McAlister is reimbursed for her losses."

I really didn't know what the hell to say. I'd expected some help from the army, but this popinjay acted like the whole thing was no affair of the military.

"How about them boys out there now? Will you be sending some soldiers out there to help them? Hadn't been for being worried about Miss McAlister, I'd still be out there."

He shook his head. "As I said before, I simply cannot help in any way. Those men are out there at their own risk and volition. I'm sorry, I just don't have the men!"

Taking a sheet of paper from a drawer, he trimmed a fresh quill and dipped it in an inkwell. Pen poised, he spoke.

"I'll need your name, also, and whatever rank you hold as a peace officer. I know this paperwork must be a bother; it certainly is to me. However . . ."

When I told him my name and added that I wasn't an officer, but rather a sort of trouble-shooter, he leaned back and opened another drawer. "This message came from Camp Hudson, and it's addressed to you. Sounds rather important, so perhaps you should read it right away." He handed it to me.

COME HOME NOW—CARLOS AND LYSANDER BAD HURT—
SOME MEN DEAD—SAME LIKE WAR—NEED YOUR HELP—
NO WANT LOSE MILO—SIGNED—ABIGAIL McCOWAN—CAMP
HUDSON.

"The wires are down now," he told me. "However, that was
received two days ago. Is she your wife?"

I looked up at him. "No, sir, she's my mother." I shook
my head. What could I do now? Ada was lying in the hospital
all shot up, and gosh knows how long she'd have to be in
there. Draining the whiskey in the glass, I stood up with my
hat in my hand and stared at the colonel.

"Would there be any way I could buy a coupla horses here
on the post," I asked. "And I'll need some grub and also a
handgun of some sort, a .44. I left mine back there."

"What about Miss McAlister?" He was standing up, also,
a puzzled look on his face. "Are you planning to just go and
not even leave some sort of message for Miss McAlister?" His
expression and tone were incredulous, and I figgered that at
last I'd broken through his brittle façade.

"I ain't much on writing, colonel," I told him. "But I'd be
obliged to you if you'd just tell her that I'll be back, and as
soon as I can. I'll know where to find her!"

On my way out of the gate, I paused and looked back. My
fine chestnut horse was all doctored up, following along behind
on a lead with the pack horse. I knew Ada would understand,
and perhaps I could come back soon.

The trail south would lead right through the scene of our
encounter with them Injuns, and mebbe I'd find sign of Garth
and the rest of them. Knowing Red, I was sure he'd survived
that ruckus if there'd been any possible way to do it. But if he
and the others had died, what better way to go? When a man
takes a gun in his hand and heads out into some wild, untamed
country, he has to play by the rules.

AUTHOR'S NOTE

THE COMPLETION OF A TRANSCONTINENTAL RAIL-road sounded the death knell of cross-country stagecoach lines but failed to solve the transportation problems of those who lived off the main line. At least not until the automobile became common property to those who could afford them.

Well into the 1930s, stages still hauled rural dwellers, but in many cases those stages were merely wagons. Driven by rugged, sunburned, capable men, they serviced remote towns near operating mine sites and isolated cattle ranches. The rock slide, the flash flood, and the prairie fire remained, too often, constant danger to those who drove the narrow, rutted stage roads.

Although Union Pacific's rails had reached Cheyenne early in November of 1867, Wells Fargo continued to operate stages in portions of Nebraska, Colorado, and other states west of the Mississippi River. Some short-distance lines, a nuisance to the large conglomerate, were leased or taken over by bold and enterprising individuals who didn't know the meaning of the word "quit"! One such venture was the fictitious company Forney & McAlister (circa 1868) herein portrayed.

Robert Bell
Creek Park Ranch
October 1983

About the Author

A true westerner by birth, Robert Vaughn Bell grew up in the Nebraska cattle country. His obvious knowledge of the early days of the American west, and his feeling for the adventurous men and women who settled there, is very apparent in his authentic description of the terrain, the equipment, and the people. Bell's writings include many magazine articles, and three other western novels, all published by Ballantine. He and his wife, Billie, reside on their Creek Park Ranch, high in the foothills of the California Sierras, where they raise beef cattle, and continue research for his books.